by LISA FIEDLER and anya wallach

Concept by Anya Wallach

PUBLISHED BY SLEEPING BEAR PRESS

Copyright © 2015 Lisa Fiedler
Copyright © 2015 Anya Wallach

Library of Congress Cataloging-in-Publication Data

Fiedler, Lisa. Curtain up / written by Lisa Fiedler and Anya Wallach.
pages cm. -- (Stagestruck ; book 1)
Summary: After twelve-year-old Anya fails to make the soccer team, she
decides to pursue her true passion, musical theater, and, with the help
of her sister and new friend Austin, pulls together a summer theater troupe.
ISBN 978-1-58536-923-2 (hard cover) -- ISBN 978-1-58536-924-9 (paperback)
[1. Theater--Fiction. 2. Musicals--Fiction. 3. Friendship--Fiction. 4.
Sisters--Fiction. 5. Community life--Fiction.] I. Wallach, Anya. II.
Title.
PZ7.F457Cs 2015
[Fic]--dc23
2014035452

ISBN 978-1-58536-923-2 (case)
1 3 5 7 9 10 8 6 4 2

ISBN 978-1-58536-924-9
1 3 5 7 9 10 8 6 4 2

Cover design by Jeanine Henderson

Printed in the United States.

Sleeping Bear Press™

2395 South Huron Parkway, Suite 200
Ann Arbor, MI 48104

© 2015 Sleeping Bear Press
Visit us at sleepingbearpress.com

Hello!

The story you are about to read really did happen. Well, not everything exactly the way it's written, but in 1995, I did create the Random Farms Kids' Theater. And it's still around today! Only now it's become this internationally recognized organization. If you had asked my younger self if I ever could have imagined that happening, well, I probably would have said that I could imagine it, but I'd never have believed it would *actually* happen.

You'll read in this book how it all worked out, but let me skip to something you won't read about.

In a local newspaper article that was printed a few weeks after our first show, it said "Though her directorial debut was a success, Anya said she is unlikely to again take on such a responsibility in the near future." Of course, reading that now makes me laugh. Running Random Farms became my

career. And now I see Random Farms kids everywhere—when I turn on the TV, see a movie, or (my favorite) go to a Broadway show. They make me proud, and it gives me the chills when I remember our humble beginnings.

When I was growing up, I wasn't the smartest or the fastest or the most popular. I didn't have any special skills, besides just really loving theater. I just made stuff up as I went along, even when people thought I was kind of crazy or told me it was impossible. I hope you will be inspired when you read this—inspired to do whatever it is that *you* imagine. Because that's how things do happen.

Curtain Up!
Anya

CHAPTER

"Anya, look out!"

I spun around just in time to see the black-and-white comet barreling toward my head.

I dropped to the ground, hearing the whoosh of the soccer ball as it zoomed over my ponytail. A split second later it landed with a thud in the grass about ten yards beyond me.

Great, I thought, *I may have avoided a concussion, but I just made a total fool out of myself in front of the entire soccer team!*

As if to confirm it, someone from the sidelines started to giggle; then someone else said, "Shhh," but I could tell the shusher herself was trying not to giggle. That would be Daria Benson, the rising team captain and without a doubt the coolest girl at Chappaqua Middle School. Daria was one of those girls who matched her lip gloss and eye shadow to her soccer uniform. Meanwhile, I didn't even know it was acceptable to wear lip gloss and eye shadow with a soccer uniform.

What am I doing here? I wondered. Because seriously, I had absolutely no delusions about my athletic ability. I liked sports, and I wasn't completely uncoordinated, but I was definitely not a natural-born jock. The only reason I'd agreed to try out for the soccer team in the first place was because my best friend, Becky Mezan (who *was* a natural-born jock, maybe even a natural-born *super*jock), had talked me into it. And to be honest, if a person were going to be stuck in middle school with the Daria Bensons of the world, wouldn't it better to be on their team . . . literally?

But as I reached up to remove a clump of dirt from my hair, I realized there were about a zillion other places I'd rather be right now. My first choice would be New York City, at a Broadway theater, watching *Aladdin* or *Newsies* or even *Wicked* again (I'd already seen it twice, but so what? I would go again in a heartbeat!).

Across the field, somebody asked, "Is she alive?"

I opened my eyes and saw Becky staring down at me, looking pretty concerned. She was the one who'd shouted the warning that had kept me from being decapitated by the speeding soccer bomb. As she reached down to help me to my feet, I could feel everyone's eyes on me. I suppose I should have been thanking Becky for saving my life, but at the moment, with all the other sixth- and seventh-grade soccer hopefuls (not to mention Daria and the rest of the returning players) staring at me, being decapitated suddenly didn't seem like such a bad thing after all.

"Are you okay?" Becky whispered, and then grimaced. "Um, you've got some grass stuck . . . right there . . ." Mortified, I sputtered the grass pieces from my lip.

"Okay, everybody," said Daria, swinging her thick auburn braid and smiling around at the twenty-two of us who'd come to try out for the team. "Coach says we can wrap it up. Awesome job today! As you know, we can pick only six new girls for next year. The new team members will be posted outside the gym first thing tomorrow morning. Good luck, you guys!"

With that, Daria and her glittering circle of athletically gifted besties turned and sauntered back to the school building. The other candidates broke into groups and pairs and walked off, chattering excitedly about what they thought their chances were of making the team. A couple of girls turned to peek at me over their shoulders and chuckle.

I wanted to dig a hole right in the middle of the center circle and crawl in.

"Don't worry about it," said Becky, reading my mind as she hoisted her hot pink, glitter-encrusted gym bag onto her shoulder. "By tomorrow everyone will forget what happened."

"Which part?" I grumbled. "The part where I fell on my face, or the part where I had to spit grass clippings out of my mouth?"

"Both," Becky assured me with a smile.

I seriously doubted it, and Becky could tell from my expression.

"Well, if they don't," she continued, "it's no big deal. Tomorrow's the last day of school anyway, and once the roster's posted, nobody will give the soccer team a second thought until September."

Becky would make the team, no question. She was that flawless combination of girly-girl and superjock (did I mention the glittery gym bag?), and half the boys in school had crushes on her. My best friend was basically a perfect human being, which, when you were twelve, was the kind of thing that either totally impressed you—or made you sick to your stomach. If I were going to be truthful about it, I'd have to say in my case, it was a little of both.

"Too bad there's no middle-school theater program," she said with a sigh. "That would be great for you."

"Yeah," I grumbled. Then I stopped walking and turned

4

to look at her. "Why don't they? Have a theater program, I mean."

"I don't know." Becky shrugged. "They have one at the high school."

True, but that meant I wouldn't get to do a play until I got to Chappaqua Central High, and that was two years away. The thought of having to wait until I was a freshman in high school to do anything theatrical was pretty depressing.

"Let's go get pizza or something," I suggested when we reached the front of the school.

"Can't," said Becky. "I've got swim practice and then a diving lesson, and after that I'm meeting my brother for golf."

I smiled. This was pretty much a typical Becky Mezan daily schedule. I'd forgotten she'd joined the town's summer swim team, and I felt a twinge of sadness because I knew that all the swim practicing and competing would take up a lot of her summer vacation time.

We said our good-byes, promised to Skype later, and she went to meet her mother in the parking lot while I headed to the side entrance of the school to await the late bus.

Ugh. Late Bus. Honestly, are there two more horrendous words in the entire English language?

A handful of kids were already assembled there—some of the soccer hopefuls who'd witnessed my embarrassment,

Kevin something-or-other who spent pretty much every afternoon in detention, and a few student council members who'd stayed late to decorate the gym for tomorrow night's eighth-grade semiformal dance.

And Austin Weatherly was there.

That was weird. Austin was in my grade. We didn't know each other well, but I did know that he lived only one block from school. That was the weird part, because why would he be waiting for the late bus when he could just walk home?

I got my answer when I saw that Mrs. Warde was the Late Bus Duty Teacher today.

Mrs. Warde was head of the English Department and pretty much everyone's favorite teacher. And since everyone knew that Austin Weatherly was the best writer in the sixth grade, maybe even the whole school, it made perfect sense to me that he was there to discuss something with the most creative teacher on the faculty. Austin was the sort of guy a lot of girls would overlook, but I'd always kind of noticed him. I didn't have a lot of experience with boys (the overlook-able type or otherwise), but it seemed to me a smart, quiet guy would be much easier to be yourself around than one of those high-profile guys who thinks a varsity jacket actually passes for a personality.

"I agree with you completely, Austin," Mrs. Warde was

saying. "And I think your idea to form a drama club for next year is brilliant. Really, I do." She paused to stop Kevin what's-his-name from pickpocketing one of the student council kids.

Talk about timing! Maybe this was what was known as kismet. Or karma? Or maybe just dumb luck. Whatever it was, my heart did a happy little somersault in my chest. I had just been wishing for a drama club, and now Austin was getting the school to start one!

But then Mrs. Warde turned back to Austin. "I'm so sorry, Austin. I presented your idea to Principal Morris, but unfortunately, there's just no room in the student budget at this time."

Austin looked utterly defeated.

"I would love to provide you with an outlet for the musical you're writing," the teacher continued, "but there's just nothing I can do." She gave him a warm smile, the kind that made kids like one teacher better than all the others. "Tell you what, though. If you make any headway on your play over the summer, shoot it to me in an e-mail. I'd be more than happy to read it and tell you what I think."

Austin thanked her, but he still seemed pretty bummed.

I, on the other hand, was kind of amazed. Austin Weatherly was writing a musical? That was pretty ambitious for a sixth grader.

I thought about telling him so, but that was when the late bus pulled up and Mrs. Warde had to get down to business, herding us into a single-file line and making sure Kevin whatever-his-name-was sat somewhere up front where the bus driver could keep an eye on him.

As I flopped onto my own seat, I watched Austin through the window, skulking off across the parking lot. I knew exactly how he felt.

In the next moment I heard myself cry out, "Stop the bus, please!"

The driver hit the brakes, and the big yellow vehicle squealed to a halt. I popped up from my seat, bolted up the aisle, and thanked the driver when he opened the door and let me out onto the sidewalk.

Then, barely able to believe I was doing it, I turned and ran off after Austin Weatherly.

I had a proposition for him!

☆⭐☆

I caught up to Austin just before he turned the corner onto his street.

"Austin!" I called. "Wait up!"

He stopped walking to glance over his shoulder, and

when he saw me, a very confused expression came over his face. I suppose this was because I had never really spoken to him before in my life (except once in third grade when I'd lent him an orange gel pen and he'd said, "Thank you" and I'd said, "You're welcome"), and suddenly here I was sprinting down the street after him, shouting his name.

Or maybe I still had grass stuck to my face.

"Hey," I said when I reached him. "So . . . I was listening . . . I mean, well, I wasn't really *listening*—it was more like I just happened to overhear what you were saying to Mrs. Warde back there. Ya know, about a drama club? Starting one . . . next year? At school?"

"Oh, right." Austin nodded. "I just thought it would be fun. Plays can be really cool."

I was momentarily sidetracked by how different his voice was from how it had sounded the time he'd thanked me for that pen.

"I totally agree," I said. "My family goes to at least two Broadway shows a year, and back in elementary school I played Mouse Number One in the fifth-grade production of *Cinderella*."

"I remember that," said Austin. "Didn't one of the mice mess up the dance number and Sophia Ciancio almost trip over his tail?"

9

"Right!" I giggled, picturing it. "And Sophia was so mad, she tried to push poor Mouse Number Three off the stage and into the orchestra pit."

"Luckily, you grabbed the back of his coat before he landed on the oboe player." Austin shook his head, smiling. "What ever happened to Mouse Number Three?"

"Not sure," I said, shrugging. "I think he transferred to a private school right after the tail incident."

Then Austin and I stood there for, like, a zillion years waiting for one of us to figure out what to say or do next. Austin shifted his weight from one foot to the other, and I tugged on the end of my dark brown ponytail. He took off his metal-rimmed glasses and put them on again.

"I'd like to read your play," I blurted out finally.

He looked confused again. "Why?"

Because there's no way I'm going to make the soccer team, that's why, I thought. *And freshman year is forever from now.* But I didn't want to say that out loud. "I have an idea," I replied instead. Austin went from confused to curious.

His blue eyes behind his glasses seemed very interested. "What is it?"

To tell the truth, I wasn't sure. Not completely, not yet. All I knew was that the idea was starting in the back of my brain, and it was on its way to being amazing.

Chapter One

"Let's go grab a cup of coffee," I said, smiling at Austin. "My treat."

We walked three blocks to Main Street. It was just the amount of time I needed to formulate the basic principles of my big idea. By the time we'd reached the coffeehouse, I was ready to make my pitch.

I held the door open for Austin. "After you," I said.

"Um, I should probably tell you," he said, stepping inside. "I don't drink coffee."

"Me either. I was just using it as a euphemism for sitting down together and having a chat."

Austin grinned. "A euphemism, huh?"

As planned, my use of writing terminology had impressed him.

We grabbed two sodas out of the cooler, paid, then found a table by the window and sat down. At this time of day the coffeehouse was pretty empty except for an older couple eating scones, and a few high-school kids who were trying to seem grown-up by drinking soy and skim double lattes and other drinks I couldn't pronounce.

As I watched Austin twist the cap off of his soda bottle, I noticed that behind those glasses, his eyes were even bluer than I'd realized. I opened my own and took a drink.

"So, what's this idea of yours?" Austin asked, sipping his soda.

"Well, it's kind of still in the planning phases," I admitted. "But Becky Mezan and I were talking earlier—"

"Becky Mezan, huh?" I noticed Austin was blushing. I have to admit: I wished he weren't. So, here was another boy who was crazy about my BFF. I decided not to think about that at the moment. I also decided that if Austin's name ever came up in conversation with Becky, I might refrain from mentioning how blue his eyes were.

"Well . . . ," I began. "We were talking about the fact that our school doesn't have a theater program, and how crummy that is for kids like me"—I motioned to him with my straw—"and you, too, actually—who really like that sort of thing."

"Agreed," said Austin. "Although, I have to say, I never realized you were so into drama. I thought maybe the mouse thing had been a fluke."

I shook my head. "Not a fluke at all. I've always been a

theater geek. In fact, my most prized possession is a Playbill from *Wicked*, signed by the entire Broadway cast. My dad had gotten it for me at some charity auction, and he'd given it to me with a bouquet of roses after *Cinderella*. I'd almost cried when I'd seen Kristen Chenoweth's name! When Sophia had heard about it, she'd had a fit and tried to get her dad to buy her an autographed Playbill too. Sophia's mom had told my mom that Dr. Ciancio had tried for weeks, but he couldn't get his hands on one." I paused, remembering how, at the time, I'd secretly been glad about having something Sophia didn't. "But the point is, *Cinderella* was actually my second performance. Before that, I was in a regional production of *Annie*. It was kind of a big deal. We even had some professional actors in the cast. Auditioning for that was one of the most exhilarating experiences of my life!"

"Were you Annie?"

"Actually, I was an orphan in the chorus," I explained. "I didn't have any lines or solos, but I still got to sing and dance, which was awesome. My big moment was on opening night, when Miss Hannigan almost tripped over me. The good news was, I got a huge laugh. The bad news was, it wasn't supposed to happen."

Austin smiled. "That's theater for ya. Even when it goes wrong, it's still pretty incredible."

"Right!" That was *exactly* how I'd felt at the time! I couldn't believe how much this kid "got it."

"So the fifth-grade adaptation of *Cinderella* was a bit of a step backward for you," he observed.

"Well, the production was a lot less professional if that's what you mean." I shrugged. "Not to sound full of myself, but I probably could have been cast as Cinderella if I hadn't totally flubbed my lines at the audition. Sophia was watching my audition from the wings, and she picked that exact moment to have a sneezing fit. It totally distracted me."

"Interesting," said Austin. "If I remember correctly, Sophia wound up being cast as Cinderella."

I nodded. "To be fair, though, Sophia really is a talented actor."

"Talented enough to make a phony sneezing fit sound believable, at least," Austin joked.

I laughed. "But the thing is, being in those plays made me realize that I wanted to do something big in the world of theater someday. I made sure I learned all I could about everything from lighting cues to costume changes. I took in every minute of it, from the overture to the final curtain call. Although, for the record, during *Cinderella* I wasn't completely professional when it came time for us to take our bows."

Austin raised an eyebrow. "What do you mean?"

"Well, when Sophia came out to take her bow, I couldn't help myself—*I* faked a big loud sneeze!"

This cracked him up.

"It's not fair that the sporty kids in our school have a whole list of teams to choose from," I said. "And the leadership-types have student council, and there's even a science club and a chess club, but there's no drama club."

"That's why I suggested they start one," Austin said glumly. "But you heard Mrs. Warde. The school board cannot presently"—he gestured sarcastically with air quotes—" 'allocate the necessary funds' for that kind of thing."

"Well, I'm not sure what 'allocate funds' means," I admitted with a grin, "but if it's anything like shelling out the cash, don't worry about it. The club I'm thinking about has nothing to do with the school board. Or even with school, for that matter."

He frowned. "I don't understand."

I took a deep breath. "What if we put on a play ourselves?" I said, hoping to sound excited, capable, and confident all at once. "By ourselves. And not just any play, *your* play. Right away. This summer!"

"*This* summer?"

"Yes! Who needs some out-of-touch school board when we can put on your play ourselves? And if it goes well, we can do another one. And another one . . ." I forced myself to stop. I didn't want him to think I was the type who got carried away.

Austin took a long sip of his drink; his eyebrows were knit together as he mulled this over. Finally he said, "How would we do this?"

"Well, I haven't actually gotten that far yet," I confessed. "The idea just came to me this afternoon, somewhere between my crash-and-burn soccer tryout and your conversation with Mrs. Warde. But c'mon, you've got to admit—it's tempting, isn't it? We can cast it ourselves, produce it, and advertise for it. . . . I bet lots of people will want to see a world-premiere play by a local playwright, starring local kids."

I could tell he was flattered. "I like the way you think," he said with a crooked grin.

The grin made my cheeks feel warm. "Thanks."

"I want this to be an actual theater. Our own real theater, except kids do everything. Act, direct, choreograph"—I pointed to him with my straw—"write and compose!"

"That sounds amazing," said Austin. "There's just one small problem with that last part. I haven't finished writing the play yet."

"Oh." I frowned. "Well, you get straight As in English, don't you? So, how long can it take?"

"Maybe days, maybe weeks." He shrugged. "Maybe even years. That's how it is with creative writing. Some days I can barely get the words down fast enough, and other days . . . nothing."

This was what one might call a major glitch. Half a play was definitely not what I had in mind. "That certainly puts a damper on things."

"Not necessarily," said Austin. "You've still got a great idea. It would be cool to put on a musical, even if it isn't mine."

"You mean, we should put on a famous play, like *Hairspray* or *Into the Woods*?"

Austin was clearly impressed at the way I'd just rattled off these titles. "Wow. You really are an expert, aren't you?"

I gave him a modest shrug. "Aspiring theater professional, remember?" I drank a little more soda and considered his suggestion. "I really wanted to do something original," I said at last. "Something no one's ever seen before, ya know? Something new."

"I think I can still help you out," he said.

My heart thudded. "That would be awesome, Austin. But how? I wouldn't want you to rush your writing. Especially since that musical is going to be your Tour de France."

He laughed. "I think you mean my 'tour de force.' And believe me, I'd never do that. But here's the thing about writing. Even though my big musical is probably going to be a work in progress for quite a while, that doesn't mean I can't work on other projects at the same time."

"It doesn't?" I had no idea playwrights could be such multitaskers.

"Nope. Which is why I think I can help you put together something that's more suited to your needs. Something bigger than a skit but smaller than a full-on musical."

"You mean, like a theatrical revue?" I said. "Individual acts and numbers, like a cabaret?"

"Exactly."

I liked that we agreed so easily. This seemed to bode well for our professional partnership. "Okay, so, how do we make this happen?"

"I've got a pretty awesome collection of scripts and scene books and sheet music at home. I'll just pull a bunch of songs and monologues and scenes, and assemble them into a script, writing some original stuff in between to connect them."

"We've got tons of that kind of stuff too," I told him. "Including my *Annie* script from that regional production."

"It won't take long to put together something pretty great," he promised. "And it might be good for me to shift my focus for a bit."

It was all I could do to keep from throwing my arms

around him and hugging him. I could only imagine what the high-school coffee drinkers would think of *that*!

Instead we clinked bottles and finished our sodas.

"We'll have to start advertising right away," I decided. "I should go home to get started on that. Not to mention thinking about the details. Great theater is all about the details."

"Great quote," said Austin. "Who said that?"

"I did," I said, and laughed. "Just now." My heart flipped over in my chest as I summoned the courage to ask my next question. "Do you . . . um . . . want to come over to my house and . . . um . . . ya know . . . start thinking about it . . . together?"

"Sure," he said, standing up and heading for the door. "Let's go."

OMG . . . I just invited a boy with amazing blue eyes to come to my house.

And he said yes!

When we turned onto my street, Random Farms Circle, I found my little sister, Susan, hanging out with a bunch of her friends on the lawn of the old neighborhood clubhouse. It was this antique barn left over from, like, the early 1900s, when Random Farms was an actual farm. It was later renovated into a community center for the neighborhood, and for many years it hosted bridge tournaments, rummage sales, birthday parties, and bake sales. But lately it had just been sitting there, empty.

Susan and her friend Mia Kim were sitting under the tall oak tree on the clubhouse lawn. When they saw me approaching with Austin, they both stopped talking midsentence and stared. I could tell they were stunned by the fact that I was walking home with a boy. To be honest, I was pretty stunned myself.

Susan was a year younger than me, which, in the kid food chain, should have made us natural enemies. But she was pretty cool, much smarter than the average eleven-year-old, so I didn't have a problem with her most of the time. Occasionally, I actually liked hanging out with her.

Of course, also occasionally, she drove me totally nuts. As she hopped up and came sprinting across the lawn, I was hoping this wouldn't be one of those times.

"Hi, Anya." Her eyes darted meaningfully to Austin, then back to me. "So . . . what's going on?"

"Nothing," I said airily. "Austin's just coming over to talk about this idea I have." Then, before Susan could say anything embarrassing, I motioned for Austin to keep walking.

When we reached my front porch, I said, "I'm just going inside to get my computer. Be right back."

Austin sat down on a porch step, and I bolted into the house.

Minutes later I came back, laptop in hand, only to find Susan sitting beside him. "How'd the soccer tryouts go?" she asked me.

"As expected," I reported.

"Oh. Sorry."

To be honest, I'd pretty much forgotten all about my soccer disaster. My mind had been tumbling with theater thoughts the whole way home from the coffeehouse, and I was ready to start planning. All I needed was for my sister to get off the porch. But before I could tell her to leave us alone, she smiled at me.

"Austin just told me about the theater. How can I help?"

"By going back to the clubhouse and hanging around with your own friends," I said a bit snippily. I felt bad as soon as I heard the words come out of my mouth, but c'mon . . . When you were planning your first official theatrical business venture with an extremely cool boy, you wouldn't exactly want your little sister tagging along.

"I can be helpful, Anya. You know I love theater."

"Yeah," I said. "But this is serious stuff."

Susan rolled her eyes. "Look who's Hal Prince all of sudden."

"Wow." Austin laughed. "The kid knows who Hal Prince is, Anya. I think we kind of have to sign her up."

"Fine," I said with a sigh. "But you can't goof around or anything. I want my theater to be professional."

"I can be professional," she assured us. "So what show are we doing? *Bye Bye Birdie? Beauty and the Beast? Urinetown . . .*" She giggled. "*Urinetown*. Eww."

I cringed. Did my sister really just make a urine joke in front of Austin? So much for professional.

"We're going to do a musical revue," I informed her. "Austin's going to compile it, and I'm going to produce and direct."

"And I'm going to twirl flaming batons!"

"You are absolutely *not* going to twirl flaming batons. This is a serious theater, not a traveling circus."

We agreed that what we needed first was a name.

"Backstage Bunch?" Susan suggested.

"Too babyish," I said.

"Chappaqua Youth Repertory Theater?" Austin offered.

"Maybe a little too snobby."

"Yeah," said Austin. "Maybe."

I frowned, concentrating. Then it hit me: "What about the Random Farms Kids' Theater?" I said. "Except I don't want people to think this theater is a 'random' thing. Because it's not. It's extremely *not* random. It's totally intentional." I realized I was beginning to ramble, but I was getting more and more excited by the minute. "The Random Farms Kids' Theater is kind of a mouthful, so maybe later on we can just shorten it to Random Farms." I bit my lip, playing the name over again in my head. "Or maybe the Random Farms Kids. Unless . . . You don't think it sounds like a street gang or something, do you?"

Austin smiled. "No, Anya, I don't think it sounds like a street gang."

"Good, so maybe we leave *Theater* in the name for now so it's clear that's what we are. After all, the Random Farms Kids could be anything . . . a softball team, a political party, an activist group."

Susan was looking at me like I'd lost my mind, so I finished quickly with "We can shorten it later," and then I shut up.

"Advertising," said Austin, moving on. "Super-important."

We came up with an ad, which I immediately posted to the community bulletin board link on the Random Farms Neighborhood Association's website (under someone's post about a whole box of calico kittens they were giving away for free) and which Susan (aka@soozapalooza2) instantly tweeted to her ever-growing list of Twitter followers:

BE A STAR at the Random Farms Kids' Theater. Actors, singers, dancers, stage crew! Reply @soozapalooza2 for info #bigdrama #theaterrules

We also decided we might benefit from going old-school and printing out the advertisement as a paper flyer that we could distribute around town. Then we made notes about holding auditions and selling tickets, and we googled all kinds of ideas for sets and wardrobe. We also talked about turning our basement into a rehearsal space and our back deck into a terrific stage, complete with footlights and a working curtain.

"Anya, you're going to be rich!" said Susan.

"What do you mean?"

"Well, aren't you going to charge the kids to be in the show?"

"I don't think so." I looked at Austin. "Should we? I mean, even if we get really creative with costumes and set designs, we're still going to have some costs."

"True," said Austin thoughtfully. "We'll definitely need some up-front money just to get things off the ground. We might have to rent lights and sound equipment."

He had a point. I was thinking we'd earn revenue through ticket sales, but that wouldn't come until later. In the meantime, we'd need some sort of funding to run the theater.

"Maybe Mom and Dad will give you a loan," Susan suggested.

"No," I said firmly. "I want to do it myself. I don't want to borrow money. From anyone."

Susan shrugged. "I'm sure you'll think of something. Boy, I didn't realize there were so many do's and don'ts for running your own theater."

Neither did I. Unfortunately, at the moment it was feeling like there were more don'ts than do's. . . .

Do's?

Dues!

As in membership fees!

"That's it!" I cried. "We can ask the kids who join the theater to pay dues. Nothing excessive—just enough to get the ball rolling. So, we aren't really charging them; we're just asking them to contribute to the process."

"Excellent," said Austin. "Creative set design, inexpensive costumes, and membership dues. Anya, you're already thinking like a producer."

It was the best praise I could have asked for. Of course, I was also going to be the director. And I was looking forward to thinking like one of those, too.

"I think kids will be okay with paying dues," I said confidently.

We decided we'd "crunch the numbers" (as Austin put it) and come up with an exact dues amount later. The more immediate concern was figuring out who might be interested in joining our theater. We needed kids with "a flair for the dramatic" (also Austin's term).

"Well, I know at least five girls in this neighborhood who take dance," I pointed out. "They'd make a great chorus line. You know Mackenzie Fleisch, right?"

Austin cocked his head. "Is she the girl who always stands with her heels together and her feet pointing east and west?"

"Otherwise known as first position," I said, grinning, but I knew this only because I'd taken a few years of dance back in elementary school. "It's a ballet thing. Mackenzie lives for ballet. Her mom told my mom that Kenzie's going to be a prima ballerina someday."

"That's impressive."

I created a new page in my theater document and typed in the names of all the girls we knew who took dance. Then we made a second list that included everyone in the sixth-grade concert choir, and a third with the names of all the kids who'd been in the fifth-grade play with me (minus Mouse Number Three, of course), and as many as we could remember who'd been in it the year before. Susan rattled off the names of the kids who'd been in it this year.

"We're going to need more than just performers," I pointed out. "We'll need kids to handle sound and lighting and stuff like that."

"Don't worry about that," said Austin. "My friend Deon will love this idea. He can oversee all our technical needs. He won the science fair last year for making a light bulb out of a sweet potato. Or maybe it was a can opener out of an electric toothbrush. Whatever it was, I'm sure he'll be willing to help us out."

I turned to Susan. "Do you think Mia will be interested

in joining?"

"Oh yeah," said Susan, nodding hard. "Mia's an amazing singer."

"She is," I agreed. "Little girl, big voice."

"Listen to you!" Austin laughed. "You sound like a real director. What are you gonna say next? 'Don't call us, we'll call you'?"

"How about 'I'll have my people call your people'?" I teased, giggling.

"Well, now, aren't we just a happy little bunch . . ."

The cool voice had come from the street. It was a voice I knew well.

It was the voice that had beaten me out for the role of *Cinderella* a year ago.

Sophia.

CHAPTER

I quickly closed my computer as Sophia Ciancio dropped her super-expensive hot pink bicycle onto my front lawn and headed for the porch.

"Hi, Anya." Sophia swung her long dark hair over one shoulder and smiled at Austin. "Hi. You're that guy in my English class who writes all those poems, right?"

"For your information," Susan pointed out defensively, "he doesn't just write poetry. He's also writing an original musical revue for—"

I gave my little sister a firm nudge with my elbow to cut her off. But it was too late.

"Oh, right. I just saw something about that on Twitter."

Since I was pretty sure Sophia Ciancio didn't follow my sister (or anyone else who wasn't world famous or at the very least part of Chappaqua's middle-school elite popular crowd) on Twitter, I realized that someone must have already retweeted it.

Sophia laughed. "I actually thought it was a joke."

"Well, it's not," I said curtly. "We're creating a theater."

"Seriously? Where?"

"Here," I said. "At my house."

"Who's going to be in it?"

I gave her what I hoped was a careless shrug. "Just . . . ya know . . . people."

"Hmmm." Sophia treated us to another hair toss. "I might be interested in that," she said coolly. "I mean, if Austin's writing it." She actually batted her eyes at him. I kind of wanted to puke.

Then, without even saying good-bye, she sauntered back across the front yard, got on her neon bike, and glided off, calling, "Let me know the details."

Um, yeah, that *is* so *not happening*, I thought.

Back to business.

But as I opened my laptop again, I couldn't shake the feeling that I'd forgotten something.

Something big.

Then the front door opened behind me, and my mother stepped out onto the porch. She was holding her cell phone and looking very upset.

And that was when I realized that, unlike Sophia Ciancio, my mother *did* follow Susan on Twitter.

"Girls," Mom said, her eyebrows knit low. "Is there something you think I should know?"

I sighed. *That* was what I'd forgotten.

I'd forgotten to ask my parents!

Slowly, patiently, my mom folded her arms across her chest. "Anya, what exactly is the Random Farms Kids' Theater?"

Before I could answer, Dad's car pulled into the driveway.

"Hello, there," he said cheerfully as he headed up the walk. "I caught an early train."

My dad's a big important lawyer in the city and it was unusual to see him home at this time of day.

Just my luck—a slow day in the world of law.

He looked from me to my mom and became instantly wary. "What's up?"

I took a deep breath and explained my theater idea to them, just like I'd explained it to Austin.

"It'll be great, don't you think?" I finished confidently. "And I promise we won't make a mess in the kitchen or stomp on the rose bushes in the yard or swing from the chandelier in the dining room or anything like that. All I want to do is put on a play. Well, several plays, actually. But one at a time. Naturally."

Mom had a strange expression on her face. It was a mix of concern and something else. Pride, maybe? She smiled and reached out to hold my hand. "I'm sorry, Anya," she said. "I love that you're thinking so creatively and that you have such confidence in your idea. But we can't have a theater in our house."

"Well, it won't be in the house, exactly," I clarified. "It'll be in the basement, mostly. And I've thought it all out."

"Have you?" Mom cocked an eyebrow.

"Sure. . . . We've got tons of sheet music in the piano bench, and you're always complaining about the old clothes cluttering up the closets. Those would make a great start for a wardrobe department."

"And what about the fact that this house also happens to be my workplace?"

Ugh. Okay, so maybe I hadn't thought it all out. I was so excited about the theater that I hadn't even considered the fact that my mom ran her own PR consulting business, which, after I was born, she'd relocated from a giant skyscraper in New York City to the paneled den space just off our living room. She even had a separate entrance for clients so they wouldn't have to come through the house for meetings.

"Maybe your clients wouldn't mind," I offered lamely.

"They pay for my professionalism," Mom said gently.

"And I don't think I'd be able to get much work done, let alone hold any meetings with a hundred singing, dancing middle schoolers traipsing around the house."

I brightened. "You really think I'm going to get a hundred people to join my theater?"

Mom sighed. "That was just a 'for instance,' Anya," she said, handing my dad her cell to get him up to speed via Susan's tweet. "And it doesn't matter what size turnout you get. The point is, you simply can't have a children's theater in my place of business."

"So, you're saying even though Austin and Susan and I have spent the entire afternoon making plans, we can't have a theater?"

"She's not saying you can't have a theater," Dad clarified. "She's saying you can't have a theater *here*."

Same thing. I needed a place to have rehearsals and perform the show. If my own house was off-limits, that meant I was pretty much out of venue options. I turned a hopeful look to Austin.

"Sorry," he said. "My little sisters are two and four. They take naps. My parents would never agree to having a theater in our house."

"How about we take a look at the parks and rec summer program brochure," Dad suggested. "Maybe they're offering a theater camp you can join."

"No!" I sprung up from the porch step, feeling a lump forming in the back of my throat. "You don't understand. I want to do this. . . . I *need* to do this! No kid in our town has ever done anything like this before. Maybe no kid in any town has ever done it! I want to put on this play more than I've ever wanted anything in my life!"

Mom and Dad did that parent-telepathy thing where they only had to exchange one glance and each knew what the other was thinking.

Unfortunately, so did I. They were thinking no.

☆☆☆☆

Suddenly I needed to get out of there.

"Come on, Austin," I said, going down the steps. "I'll walk you home."

But I wasn't actually walking; it was more like a very furious stomp.

We were all the way to the end of Random Farms Circle when Susan caught up to us.

"Anya, wait!"

I slowed from a stomp to a heated walk. But I was too upset to stop moving entirely.

"I asked Mom if we could have rehearsals in the back-yard," she said, panting to catch her breath. "She said it might work as long as we stay outside and as far from her office window as possible."

"That might not be so bad," said Austin.

"And what if it rains?" I grumbled. "And what happens when someone needs to use the bathroom?"

"Maybe no one will," said Susan, trying to be helpful.

I rolled my eyes. "Susan, sooner or later someone's going to have to use the bathroom."

We walked on in grim silence until we reached the next block, where the old neighborhood association clubhouse stood behind a tangle of overgrown rhododendron and climbing vines. The grumpy groundskeeper, Mr. Healy, was there, pulling up dandelions.

"Don't know why I have to bother keeping up a place nobody uses," he muttered, yanking a weed and tossing it over his shoulder. "Waste of time, if you ask me."

"Who's that?" Austin whispered.

"Mr. Healy," Susan whispered back. "He takes care of all the common spaces in the neighborhood. He's kind of grouchy."

We watched Mr. Healy jerk another dandelion out of the earth and fling it into the growing pile behind him.

"Doesn't seem to enjoy his job very much," Austin noted.

"Can't blame him," I allowed. "Nobody's used the club-house in years. It seems silly to bother keeping it tidy."

"The older ladies in the neighborhood are always complaining that it's an eyesore," said Susan. "That's why the president of the Neighborhood Association insists that Mr. Healy keep the place neat."

I gave my sister a sideways look. "How do you know this?"

"Don't you ever listen when Mom talks to Mrs. Quandt next door?"

"No, I don't," I said. "Because *I'm* not a spy."

"I'm not a spy either!" said Susan. "I just like to stay in the loop."

Despite my gloomy mood, I had to smile.

As Mr. Healy continued to attack the yellow weeds and chuck them over his shoulder, my eyes went to the enormous old clubhouse building behind him. It was a giant barn with fading red paint and white trim around the large paned windows. In spite of its shoddy appearance, I could see that the building was still sturdy.

I had been inside only once, six years ago. Just before the Neighborhood Association had closed the clubhouse's doors for good, they'd used it to host an old-time ice cream social on the Fourth of July.

I could still picture the interior: a big wide-open space with great light and a tall ceiling. The contractor who'd built our subdivision had done a great job of turning it from a barn into a gathering spot. He'd added restrooms, electricity, and even a stage.

A stage! Complete with a PA system, which came in handy because somehow they'd wrangled Mr. Healy into reading the Declaration of Independence in a Thomas Jefferson costume.

There was even an old upright piano, on which one of the older neighborhood girls had played "Yankee Doodle."

Thinking back, that whole delightful day was just like a scene out of *The Music Man*.

Without warning, an idea hit me. An idea that seemed to announce itself as loudly as . . . as . . . seventy-six trombones!

"*Ye Gads!*" I cried.

"Anya," said Austin, narrowing his eyes, "Why are you quoting *The Music Man*?"

I didn't answer him.

Because I'd already taken off across the clubhouse lawn, heading straight for Mr. Healy.

Ten minutes later I returned to the curb where Austin and Susan were waiting for me, looking totally baffled.

"What was that all about?" Austin asked.

"Just a little business deal," I said, grinning. "We're going to rent the clubhouse as our theater venue."

Austin blinked. Susan's mouth dropped open.

I giggled. "Okay, well, not rent, exactly. More like barter. See, I told Mr. Healy that I . . . actually *we* . . . would be glad to take over all the clubhouse landscaping duties in exchange for being allowed to use the barn for our theater rehearsals and performance. I told him we'd clean up the inside, too."

"Anya, that's brilliant," said Susan.

Austin was shaking his head in amazement. "You really are an expert producer. This place will be perfect. And cutting the grass and sweeping out the inside is a small price to pay."

"Well, there is one slight problem," I said, stuffing my hands into the pockets of my shorts.

"How slight?" asked Susan.

"Mr. Healy says it's all right with him, but he doesn't have the final say."

"Who does?"

"The president of the Neighborhood Association does."

"Ugh." Susan, who was "in the loop," understood immediately why this constituted a problem.

"I don't get why that's an issue," said Austin, his eyes shooting from me to Susan then back to me. "Who is the president of the Neighborhood Association?"

"Dr. Ciancio," I said, letting out a long rush of breath. "Sophia's father."

CHAPTER

The next morning I hurried downstairs, eager to talk to my sister. It had taken me forever to fall asleep the night before, since my mind was reeling with ideas for the theater. At midnight Austin had texted me (a boy texting in the middle of the night? How cool was that?) to let me know he'd been working on the revue from the minute he'd gotten home. I texted back that he just might be the most dedicated playwright in the history of the universe. I got a smiley face in response.

I finally dozed off only to wake up again at three in the morning in a complete panic. What if, despite Susan's Twitter popularity, no one wanted to sign up for the Random Farms Kids' Theater?

What if I failed?

I slid into my place at the breakfast table and looked at my sister.

"So?" I asked. I was so anxious, I nearly knocked over my juice glass. "Any interest?"

Her answer was a huge smile. "Well, we aren't exactly trending worldwide, but there's definitely a buzz. Kids are retweeting and favorite-ing like crazy, and my phone's been lighting up like a fireworks display with people asking for more information, like when and where the theater's going to be."

"Hopefully, by this afternoon we'll have answers for them."

Mom was sitting at the table, drinking her second cup of coffee and reading the *New York Times*. Dad was loading the dishwasher.

"Susan and I won't be coming straight home from school today," I informed my parents. "We'll be stopping by the Ciancios' house. I need to ask Dr. Ciancio a very important question."

Mom put her newspaper down and gave me a serious look. "Anya, what's wrong? Aren't you feeling well?"

"Oh, I'm fine, Mom. It's not a medical question. It's a Neighborhood Association question."

"Since when are you interested in Neighborhood Association matters?" asked Dad.

"Since we can't have the theater in the house," I said. Then, in case that sounded snarky, I quickly added, "And since I remembered the clubhouse was vacant and actually has a stage."

"Well, now." Mom grinned. "Somebody's thinking like a producer, I see."

"We're going to trade landscaping services for permission to use the clubhouse," I explained.

"It's a win-win situation for everyone," said Susan.

"What makes you think the good doctor is going to be home on a weekday?" asked Dad.

"His office closes at noon on Fridays," said Susan. "He has a standing tennis match with the editor of the local newspaper, Ms. Bradley, at one thirty, which, according to Mrs. Quandt, he can only get away with because he's the best gastroenterologist in Chappaqua, so not offering Friday afternoon appointments really doesn't hurt his practice at all. Also, he and Ms. Bradley are now officially dating, which Mrs. Quandt thinks is a positive development, especially since his divorce from Mrs. Ciancio was so messy."

"Wow," I said, sipping my orange juice. "You really are in the loop!"

"Hmmm." Dad jiggled a drinking glass into the dishwasher's top rack. "Well, Anya, I wouldn't get your hopes up. Frank Ciancio is kind of a stickler for rules. I'm sure he'll have all kinds of concerns about insurance and liability."

"Mr. Healy told me the association has been paying for insurance on the clubhouse for the last six years," I reported. "He said it would make sense for someone in the neighborhood to get some use out of it, especially since it wouldn't cost Cranky Frankie one extra penny to let us have it."

"Anya!" my mother scolded. "That's very disrespectful."

"Anya wasn't the one who called Dr. Ciancio 'Cranky Frankie,' Mom," Susan pointed out in my defense. "Mr. Healy was."

Dad closed the dishwasher and hit the rinse-and-hold button. "I like how Healy thinks," he murmured.

Mom sighed and picked up her newspaper again. "Go to school, girls," she said. "And please, when you talk to Dr. Ciancio, remember to be polite."

I'll be polite, all right, I thought, plucking my schoolbag from the back of my chair. *I'm even prepared to beg if have to.*

I only hoped I wouldn't have to.

☆⭐☆✩

44

It was like every other last day of school of my life except for two things: one, for the first time ever, I found myself crushed into a group of girls crowded around the gym bulletin board, checking out the new soccer team roster. Becky's name was at the top of the list. Mine was nowhere to be found. No surprises there.

And two, depending on Dr. Ciancio's decision, I might be walking out of school and into a summer that promised more than just Tuesday afternoons at the town pool and Saturdays at the mall.

As Becky accepted congratulatory hugs and high fives from her new teammates, I turned and headed for the exit. I would call her later to tell her how proud of her I was, but right now I had somewhere to be.

I was just crossing the baseball diamond when I heard her voice.

"Anya! Wait up."

I turned and smiled, waiting for her to catch up (which, given her long-legged stride and natural speed, didn't take long).

"Are you okay?" she asked, tugging at the ends of her blond ponytail.

"I'm fine," I said, throwing my arms around her. "And congratulations! I knew you'd make the team."

"Thanks. But . . . but are you really upset about getting cut?"

"I think we both knew I never had a chance."

Becky gave me a curious look. "Well, if you aren't bummed about not making the team, why did you leave so suddenly?"

"Oh!" I laughed. "I need to be somewhere. I have a meeting."

"A meeting? What kind of meeting?"

"A meeting to discuss"—I flung my arms out wide in a big ta-da gesture—"my theater."

"Anya, that's great!" cried Becky. "You found a theater program!"

I grinned at her. "Not found. Found*ed*! I'm starting my own theater. Well, not by myself. Austin Weatherly's going to help me, and we're going to open it up to any kid who wants to join."

"That's amazing." Becky looked genuinely impressed and very happy for me.

"I was going to tell you about it," I explained, "but I didn't want to steal your soccer thunder. I planned on calling you tonight once Austin and I got everything figured out."

"Austin Weatherly," said Becky, her eyes dancing. "He got a lot cuter this year, didn't he?"

We could have stood there talking about Austin's upgrade

46

in cuteness for hours. But I had scheduled a rendezvous with my in-house playwright, my administrative assistant (or, as she'd dubbed herself, my as-*sister*-ant), and good old Cranky Frankie Ciancio.

"Text me after your diving lesson," I said, giving her another hug. "I'll fill you in on the whole theater thing then."

"Okay," said Becky.

"Congratulations again."

"You too. And thanks for not stealing my soccer thunder."

As I took off, I called over my shoulder, "Hey, maybe that can be your team nickname. Soccer Thunder!"

"I love it!" she shouted back. "I'll have them embroider it on my warm-up jacket!"

The last thing I heard as I rounded the corner was Becky making thunder sounds and laughing like crazy.

☆☆☆☆

Austin and I met in the middle-school parking lot then walked the three blocks in nervous silence to the elementary school, where we found a weepy Susan saying her heartfelt good-byes to her fifth-grade teacher and the school principal. Not that my sister was a suck-up or anything, but leaving the elementary school you've been in since pre-K, with the daunting prospect of middle school looming at the end of the summer, would make anybody emotional.

And speaking of daunting prospects . . .

"Do you know what you're going to say to Dr. Ciancio?" Susan asked me, wiping her eyes with the back of her hand and giving a big sniff as she fell into step between Austin and me.

"I'm just going to give him the facts and appeal to his sense of neighborliness," I said lamely.

"Good luck with that," she grumbled.

We found Dr. Ciancio in his driveway, putting his tennis bag into the trunk of his car. A woman I didn't recognize was standing beside him.

"Are you kids here to see Sophia?" he asked.

"God no," said Susan.

I gave her a sharp elbow to the ribs.

"We're here to see you, sir," said Austin. "About the clubhouse."

Dr. Ciancio closed the car trunk impatiently. "Well, you'll have to make it quick. We've got a tennis game in twenty minutes." He turned to the house and called, "Sophia! Let's get a move on!"

I smiled at the woman in case she was a member of the Neighborhood Association board. She smiled back. To my surprise, Austin reached out to shake her hand.

"You're Ms. Bradley, the editor in chief of the *Chappaqua Chronicle*, aren't you?" he said politely. "I've seen your picture in the paper."

"I am," Ms. Bradley replied sweetly. "And it's nice to know young people are taking an interest in the *Chronicle*."

Sophia came out the front door, dressed perfectly in the cutest little tennis dress I'd ever seen. Her long dark hair was pulled back into a bouncing ponytail that was tied with a crisp white ribbon.

Wonderful. The last thing I wanted to do was make my pitch to Dr. Ciancio in front of Sophia. She joined us in the driveway, twirling her tennis racquet. "Hi, Austin," she said with a bright smile.

"What is it you wanted to ask me about the clubhouse?" Dr. Ciancio prodded, checking his watch impatiently.

"Oh, uh . . . well . . ." I stood up a little straighter. "We were wondering if we might get your permission to use it."

Dr. Ciancio frowned. "Let me guess. Another Sunday afternoon ice cream social?"

I shook my head. "No, sir. In fact, we'd like to have it for the next three weeks, if we could."

"What in the world for?" asked Dr. Ciancio. "As I'm sure you know, the place hasn't been used in six years. We don't rent it out anymore."

"Which is why it's perfect for us," said Susan. "We don't have rent money."

"We were hoping we could barter our landscaping services in exchange for using the clubhouse," I said. "This way, Mr. Healy would be able to devote his energy to tending to other more popular public areas in the neighborhood."

"I still don't understand," said Dr. Ciancio, opening the driver's-side door. "What do you kids want with the clubhouse?"

Suddenly Sophia stopped twirling her tennis racquet and gasped. "I know what this is about! They want to use the clubhouse for their little theater."

"It's not going to be a 'little' theater," I said, scowling at Sophia. "We've gotten a ton of responses already." I turned back to Dr. Ciancio. "But she's half right. We want the clubhouse so my new theater can put on an original musical revue."

"That's fascinating!" said Ms. Bradley, looking every inch the newswoman she was. "A theater run by young people. What a wonderful project."

I really liked that she was calling us young people instead of children.

"Maybe it'll make a good story for the paper," I said boldly.

Ms. Bradley grinned. "Maybe it will."

Sophia was looking at me with a strange gleam in her eyes. I had the sense she was plotting something.

"We'll do all the outside work," said Austin. "And we'll clean up the inside, too. Mr. Healy said he'll check to be sure the plumbing and the electricity are still in good working order. We promise we'll take good care of the place, sir."

Dr. Ciancio sighed. "Sounds risky. What if one of you kids twists an ankle or falls off the stage? The neighborhood will be liable."

I was about to remind him about the insurance policy, but to my shock, someone else spoke up first.

Sophia!

"You should totally let them use the clubhouse, Daddy."

We all looked at her—the little tennis princess in her perfect white dress—who was smiling up at her father with the biggest puppy dog eyes I'd ever seen.

I had a sick feeling I knew where this was going.

"Of course," Sophia continued, batting her eyes and twirling her racquet, "there would just have to be one teeny tiny condition."

"What's that, sweetheart?" Dr. Ciancio asked.

"*I* get to be a member of their little theater," she said. "I get a part in the show." Susan's eyes flashed. Austin let out a groan. It was all I could do to keep from grabbing that tennis racquet out of her hands and smashing it into a million pieces on the driveway.

But I didn't do it.

Instead I turned my brightest theater producer's smile to Sophia and extended my hand professionally, just like Austin had done to Ms. Bradley. "Welcome to the theater," I said. "We'll be having our first meeting on Sunday morning. Eleven o'clock at the clubhouse."

Sophia hesitated only a second before accepting my handshake.

"Great, wonderful, okay then," said Dr. Ciancio, sliding into the driver's seat. "You've got the clubhouse. I'll fill out the paperwork. Your parents will have to sign it. Healy has the keys, so he'll see to the details. Princess, please, get in the car. You know how I loathe being late for a tennis match!"

Sophia gave me a triumphant little grin, while Ms. Bradley waved good-bye and slipped into the passenger seat.

"See you at rehearsal," Sophia said.

"Can't wait," Susan grumbled.

After Sophia got into the car, Austin, Susan, and I watched as Dr. Ciancio backed out of the driveway.

CHAPTER

There was a full minute of utter silence before they both whirled to gape at me, speaking—no, make that shouting—into my ears at the same time.

"Are you crazy?"

"You've lost your mind!"

"She'll ruin everything!"

"The girl is a diva!"

"I know," I said calmly. "But there was no way Dr. Ciancio was going to say yes until she piped up. Don't you see? Sophia did us a favor."

Susan reached over to place her palm on my forehead. "You lied to Mom. You aren't fine at all."

I swiped her hand away. "What are you talking about?"

"You must be deathly ill if you're sticking up for Sophia."

"I'm not sticking up for her. I'm merely stating the facts.

The girl can sing and act and dance. In theater that's called a triple threat. We can use someone like that."

Austin ran a hand through his hair and sighed. "That's true."

"But she's so *obnoxious!*" said Susan in a whiny voice. "And conceited. And pushy."

"I know that," I said. "But I'm thinking like a producer now. Sometimes you have to see the bigger picture. For the good of the show."

Susan shook her head sadly. "If Sophia's part of the bigger picture, I say let's crop her out."

Austin laughed. "Anya's right, Susan."

"Fine, whatever." Susan sighed and folded her arms across her chest. "Okay, so now that we have the clubhouse, what do we do next?"

"We announce that starting Sunday, Random Farms is open for business." I nodded to my sister. "Susan, you'll be in charge of the media blitz, tweeting and posting about the Random Farms Kids' Theater. Start by saying we've found a home in the clubhouse."

Susan took out her phone and tapped the screen until she'd opened the theater text thread. Then she typed exactly what I'd just said and invited any and all prospective thespians (Austin's word . . . and I *loved* it!) to join us there on

Sunday morning for our first informational meeting. Then she posted the same message to Twitter.

"Done," said Susan, hitting send with a flourish.

"Now what?" asked Austin.

"Now we go home and enjoy our first afternoon of summer vacation," I explained, "because beginning tomorrow, we've got work to do!"

We agreed to meet the next day for more planning. Then Austin left to go home and write, and Susan and I ambled back to our house. I felt a little shiver of excitement, thinking of how incredibly different this summer was going to be from all those that had come before.

Because this was going to be The Summer of the Random Farms Kids' Theater.

And I couldn't wait to get started.

The first thing I did when I woke up on Saturday was text Becky. She'd texted me the night before (long after I'd fallen asleep to visions of the shady Billy Flynn character from *Chicago* singing "Razzle Dazzle") to tell me her coach had put her in the one-hundred-meter butterfly event for Sunday's swim meet. It would be her first time swimming that race, and she couldn't sleep because she was nervous about it.

I typed: **U will totally win! I know U can do it.**

She texted back: **Thnx, Anya. Hope the theater meeting goes gr8 tomorrow!! Will try to swing by if the meet ends early enough. :)**

Then I got up and dragged my sister out of bed. She followed me downstairs, where I popped two bagels into the toaster oven.

"I'm going to make a list of the cleaning supplies we'll need to take to the clubhouse," I said. "We'll have to use whatever Mom has here, but we're going to promise to replace them as soon as we have the dues money."

"I'll go out to the garage and take an inventory of yard tools," said Susan, opening the fridge and grabbing a tub of cream cheese, which she placed in front of me on the breakfast bar. "Did you get a look at those flower boxes under the clubhouse windows? Nightmare!" Then she marched out of the kitchen, calling, "Don't burn my breakfast!" over her shoulder.

☆✫☆

I was halfway through my everything bagel and a quarter way through my list of cleaning products when the doorbell rang at ten fifteen. I was so caught up in making my list that I just went and answered the door without thinking about what I was wearing. It wasn't until I saw the weird look on Austin's face that I remembered I was still wearing my pink polka dot pajama bottoms and a ratty old New York Giants T-shirt. Was it my imagination or was he blushing slightly at seeing me in my pj's? I'm sure I was blushing, and *way* more than slightly.

"Um, come on in," I said, feeling like a total dork. "I'll . . . be right back."

Then I bolted upstairs, quickly changed into cutoff shorts and a *Mama Mia* T-shirt, and whipped my hair into a high ponytail. I brushed my teeth and hurried back down to the living room, where Susan had joined Austin. They were seated on the sofa, looking at her phone and all the theater-related texts and tweets.

My sister grinned at me. "Austin here was just telling me he never knew you were a Giants fan."

I would have slugged her, but that would have meant I'd be out one media specialist, so I let it slide.

Austin held out a neatly bound stack of papers. "Here's the script."

My eyes scanned the cover page.

RANDOM ACTS OF BROADWAY

Produced and Directed by
ANYA WALLACH

Written by
Austin Weatherly

Presented by
The Random Farms Kids' Theater

Talk about chills! Just seeing that phrase in print—
Directed by Anya Wallach—literally gave me goose bumps.
The first page was a list of the performance selections:

RANDOM ACTS OF BROADWAY

OPENING NUMBER
"Comedy Tonight" from A FUNNY THING
HAPPENED ON THE WAY TO THE FORUM
(Full Cast)

"Anything You Can Do"
from ANNIE GET YOUR GUN

"Seize the Day" from NEWSIES

Scene from PETER PAN

"Maybe" from ANNIE

"Try to Remember" from THE FANTASTICKS
(Dance Solo)

Monologue from YOU'RE A GOOD MAN,
CHARLIE BROWN

CLOSING NUMBER
"There's No Business Like Show Business"
from ANNIE GET YOUR GUN (Full Cast)

CURTAIN CALL TBA
(Full Cast)

I flipped through the script. In addition to the lines from the actual plays, between each number Austin had written original dialogue that would serve to introduce and connect each individual performance. It had a fun new-millennium-vaudeville vibe, which was exactly what I'd imagined when he first suggested it.

"I can't believe you already finished it," I said. "You started only two days ago."

"That's how the creative process is," he reminded me with a grin. "Sometimes things just want to be written. And besides, I can't really take that much credit. Most of it—the music, the scenes—is stuff other people have already written. I just sort of cobbled it together. "

"Well, you're a great cobbler. You made excellent choices, and it has a really good flow. Perfect songs, awesome scenes . . ." I looked up from the pages to smile at him. "Austin, you're incredible!" Then I caught myself and clarified, "I mean, this *script* is incredible."

"Thanks, Anya."

"So . . . what's the closing song?"

He crooked a grin at me. "That's a surprise."

Before I could press him for a clue, he hurried on.

"I have most of the sheet music for the songs I picked out," he added, nodding toward a pile of music books he'd placed on the coffee table. "But not all of it."

"I bet we have whatever you're missing," I assured him, hurrying across the room to the piano. I held the script reverently, just as I would handle the antique crystal gravy boat my nana Adele uses only for Thanksgiving dinner—like it

60

was priceless. Because it was.

I opened the piano bench and began rifling through all the old sheet music tucked inside. Susan and Austin came over to help me.

We laughed when I pulled out our beginner books (Ugh! "Hot Cross Buns"! Why?), and Susan found a bunch of classical compositions (which I'd always found challenging, but Susan had breezed through them like a champ).

Things improved significantly when we found my beloved Marvin Hamlisch (best composer *ever*! *A Chorus Line* . . . enough said!). Lucky for our miniscule dues-only budget, we'd collected plenty of Broadway music over the years. Much of it was from what my dad would call the "old standards," like *Guys and Dolls*, *Finian's Rainbow*, *The Fantasticks*, and *West Side Story*. Susan turned up her nose at the Gilbert and Sullivan stuff, but I confessed that I didn't mind *The Pirates of Penzance*, and this had us giggling as we belted out a few choruses of "I Am the Very Model of a Modern Major-General."

We also had an excellent cross section of newer songs from more contemporary shows like *Matilda*, *The Book of Mormon*, and *Hairspray*.

Austin was pleased with the haul; between our two collections we had music for every song in the show and plenty of additional choices for the kids to audition with. We both agreed that the more recent shows would be our best bets for the audition songs. We picked "Popular" from *Wicked* and "Seize the Day" from *Newsies*, then threw in "Maybe" from *Annie* because . . . well, because it's *Annie!*

"Who's going to provide the musical accompaniment for the auditions?" Susan asked, making a big show of cracking her knuckles.

"I guess you and Austin could take turns," I said.

"Good," said Susan, sitting down and placing her fingers on the keys. "I'll practice."

"What about the acting auditions?" I asked Austin. "Any ideas?"

"I've got a few things in mind," he said. "I e-mailed them to you last night."

"Cool. My laptop's in the kitchen. C'mon."

We left her seated at the piano and headed for the kitchen. A few seconds later we heard "Seize the Day" wafting from the living room.

Austin and I each settled onto a counter stool at the breakfast bar, and I opened my computer. I logged in to my e-mail and found that Austin had really done his homework. He'd sent me a bunch of possibilities for the acting auditions, which we quickly narrowed down to two monologues (one for girls, one for boys) and two scenes to be performed by partners. He'd picked out a perfect array of material. Dramatic, comedic, and just the right level of difficulty.

In the living room Susan had started singing along with her own accompaniment.

A chill raced up my spine as I suddenly realized that the Random Farms Kids' Theater really was my way of seizing the day! Me and all the other kids who loved to sing and act and dance, who wanted to share our talents and learn more about the incredible world of musical theater. I was grabbing my moment and making something happen. I was so lost in Susan's voice and my own thoughts that I almost didn't hear what Austin was saying.

"—dance?"

I snapped out of my reverie and looked at him, blinking. "You dance?"

He laughed. "Not at all. But I did include an ensemble dance number in the show, so I guess you're going to have to come up with some choreography for the dance audition."

By now Susan had quit practicing and was standing in the kitchen doorway. "Did someone say choreography?"

I ignored her and kept my eyes on Austin. "Oh, you mean something big and flashy, like from *42nd Street*, or *A Chorus Line*?"

"Well, maybe not quite that complicated, but yeah." Austin shrugged. "Something along those lines."

"Okay," I said, sliding down from my counter seat. "Let's get to it."

"Maybe you didn't hear me," said Austin pointedly. "I don't dance."

Susan sighed, mimed her thumb and pinkie into a pretend phone, and held it her ear. "Hello? Radio City Musical Hall? Yeah, I was wondering, could I possibly rent the Rockettes for a couple of weeks? Thaaaaat's right... the whole kick line!"

Austin laughed as Susan "hung up" the phone.

"Radio City says no," she reported wryly.

Personally, I didn't think it was funny. I had a moment of worry that maybe neither of my co-producers was taking things quite as seriously as I was. "Look," I said, "I'm hoping Mackenzie is going to sign up for this theater, and once she does, we can ask her to be the official choreographer for the show. But if we're going to have the kids perform a dance combination at auditions, we're just gonna have to come up with something ourselves. Maybe we can get ideas for a dance routine from YouTube. If we find something that inspires us, then we can revise it to make it our own original choreography."

Susan plopped herself onto the barstool, put her fingers

on the keys of my computer, and typed in "YouTube.com." We only had to search for a few minutes to discover that our best resource would be videos of the dance numbers performed at the Tony awards over the years. There we could study entire dances featuring actual Broadway stars—with the glitzy bonus of seeing them in full costume.

By unanimous vote we chose the dance performed by the cast of *How to Succeed in Business Without Really Trying* at the awards ceremony. The song was "Brotherhood of Man." Susan swooned a little over Daniel Radcliffe (and who could blame her!).

We watched the dance through from start to finish twice, then began the process of creating our own steps to simulate the style. This required space, so we moved not only the barstools but the kitchen table as well.

"Instant dance studio," I said. "Now, let's do the simplest sixteen counts."

"Yes," said Susan. "I think Austin will appreciate that."

"Me?" Austin frowned. "Why do I have to learn it?"

"So you can help my sister demonstrate tomorrow."

"Why can't you?"

"I'm the administrative arm of this organization," Susan said haughtily. "I'm going to be busy."

"Busy doing what?" Austin wanted to know.

To be honest, I was a little curious myself.

"Oh, ya know . . . counting the dues money . . ." She began ticking off a list on her fingers. "Filing paperwork, organizing the sheet music for the singing auditions, general crowd control . . ."

This was all news to me. Not that these weren't important tasks, but Susan and I had never discussed the fact that she'd be the one to handle them. And why would she just happen to be handling them during dance auditions?

Before I could mention this, my sister turned away from Austin and gave me a great big wink! Suddenly I knew exactly what she was doing—she was setting it up so that Austin and I would have to dance together.

For the second time that day I wanted to knock her out.

And, just the tiniest bit, I kind of wanted to hug her.

"Plus," she continued, "I'll be making sure there are paper towels in the clubhouse bathrooms, planning ticket sales, making sure all the folding chairs are in good working order . . ."

Okay, now she was just making things up. Still, I had to admire her creativity.

"Fine, fine," said Austin, cutting her off. "I'll do the dance demo." He gave me a nervous smile. "Just don't expect too much. I'm not exactly light on my feet."

"It's not difficult," I promised. "Watch."

I began to call out the steps as I did them. "Heel, heel, heel, twist, twist . . . and turn, heel, heel, heel . . . twist, twist, arms!"

I looked over at Austin, who tried to copy what I'd just done.

He took out a counter stool and the cookie jar.

"Don't worry about it," Susan told him breezily. "There's never any cookies in there anyway."

"Try it again," I advised.

He did. Much better.

"Now . . . knee, knee, twist, twist . . . arms up . . . box step . . . That's it!"

Austin beamed. "Hey, I think I'm getting the hang of it."

"You are! Now slide, slide. . . ."

He slid. Unfortunately, he slid right into the refrigerator, elbowed the ice dispenser, and sent an avalanche of ice cubes clattering to the floor.

"All right then," said Susan, sighing. "Austin, *you* handle the folding chairs. *I'll* do the dance demo."

I hated to admit it, but it sounded like a good idea. Not only for the good of the show but for the good of Mom's kitchen, as well.

CHAPTER

I put Austin to work creating what Susan had alluded to as "the paperwork." In all honesty, I hadn't thought about that until she'd made it up, but we were going to need to get some stuff in writing. For example, we'd need to gather information on everyone who was cast in the show—addresses, phone numbers, emergency contacts (although I sincerely hoped we wouldn't need to use those). I'd also need to get a feel for the level of prior theater experience the kids would be bringing to the project. Professional actors and dancers would have a headshot and a résumé to present at a casting call. But I wasn't likely to see any of those.

I told Austin what I was thinking, and he said he'd come up with some kind of questionnaire designed to give us the info we'd need.

"I just thought of something," said Susan. "Are you auditioning kids to see who should have what part in the show, or to see who gets to be *in* the show at all?"

"What do you mean?"

"I mean, is everyone who signs up automatically in, like the parks and rec co-ed softball team? Or is it going to be more like middle-school soccer, where some people make the cut and others get the 'thanks, but we've decided to go in another direction' line?"

I looked at her. "Another direction?"

"Yeah. Isn't that what show biz types say when they really mean 'you have no talent'?"

She was kind of right. "Another direction" was code for "we're going to pick someone else." I bit my lip. "You mean like the old, 'don't call us, we'll call you' brush-off."

Susan nodded.

"That's a good question," said Austin.

I took a moment to consider it. I hated the idea of making anyone feel like they weren't good enough, but I wanted my show—our show—to be as awesome as possible. And I'd *seen* those parks and rec softball games. . . .

"I think we should only take kids who are truly talented," I said. "Don't you guys?"

I glanced at Austin. He shrugged. Susan looked equally undecided.

But I was the director, so the decision was ultimately mine to make.

"We've decided to go in another direction," I said, practicing the line. "So, thanks, but don't call us, we'll call you."

Somewhere deep down, I didn't really like the way those words sounded. But if it were for the good of the show, then I would just have to get used to it.

"Okay," I said, "let's take it from the top."

On Sunday morning I jumped out of bed with every Broadway tune I'd ever heard spinning in my head. I would be meeting Austin at the clubhouse at ten, where we would pick up the key from Mr. Healy. Susan had texted and tweeted that sign-ups and auditions would begin promptly at eleven o'clock.

First we'd have our Welcome to Random Farms meeting, where I would explain that this was not just some goofy summer activity but a real, actual, as-professional-as-it-can-possibly-be theater. I planned to sound friendly, but very directorial, so that everyone would know I was in charge.

I liked the idea of being in charge. I was also a little bit terrified of it. Theater is like that, I realized. It has a way of making you feel everything at once.

I banged on Susan's door. "Get up!" I called. "Big day."

"Uuuuuhhhhhhhnnnnnnnnnggggg" was her reply. Susan was never much of a morning person.

I practically skipped downstairs to make breakfast.

Neatly tucked into my backpack and waiting by the front door was my laptop and one of Dad's legal pads with a pen clipped to it (old-school again!). There were also the questionnaires Austin had printed out, along with the scenes and monologues and lyric sheets. In just one hour Susan and I would hop in the car, and Mom would drive us the short distance to the clubhouse so we wouldn't have to lug all the rakes and hedge clippers and cleaning products we'd need to clean up the place after auditions. I would have liked to have gotten that task out of the way yesterday, but by the time we'd finished with the choreography and the paperwork, there hadn't been time. We'd just have to apologize to the actors for the condition of the venue and assure them that by the time they returned the next day to start rehearsals, it would look terrific.

Of course, those who wouldn't be returning for rehearsals wouldn't have that pleasure.

I pushed the thought out of my head and started humming to myself as I opened the fridge and grabbed a carton of orange juice.

"That's appropriate," Susan grumbled, padding sleepily into the kitchen.

"What is?"

"The song you're humming."

I laughed, because I hadn't even realized what it was: "I Want to Be a Producer."

It seemed like a lifetime had passed before we were finally climbing into Mom's car and heading to the clubhouse.

Make that . . . the theater.

I was happy to see Austin already sitting on the front steps. He hurried over to the car to help us unload the yard tools and cleaning stuff.

"Mr. Healy came by," he informed me, holding up the key.

My heart skipped a beat when he handed it to me, although it was hard to say whether it was because I was receiving the key to my very own theater or because Austin's fingertips brushed against mine as I took it.

I fitted the key into the rusted lock, turned the knob, and gave the oversize door a gentle push. It swung inward, creaking on its hinges. I peeked inside. I knew this was a moment I would remember for the rest of my life.

There, at the far end of the big barn, was the stage, empty and dusty, and filled with promise.

"Let's see!" cried Susan, slipping past me, her broom

propped on her shoulder. Two steps in, she stopped short, just staring. "Wow, Anya," she said softly. "This is . . . this is . . ."

"Real," I said.

It was the only word that came to mind.

It was the only word that would do.

☆⁂☆☆

Mackenzie Fleisch was the first to arrive.

"Kenzie!" I cried. "I'm so glad you're here."

"Me too," said Mackenzie. "I was totally psyched when I saw Susan's tweet. I think an all-kids theater is a great idea." She looked around at the worse-for-wear clubhouse space, and I could tell she wasn't overly impressed. "What are you calling this place?"

"Personally," said Susan, "I call it, 'the place where Mom doesn't have her office.'"

"The Clubhouse Theater has a nice ring to it," I said, coming up with it off the top of my head. "We're going to clean it up this afternoon," I added quickly. "And redecorate."

"So . . . ," said Susan, folding her arms and giving Kenzie a challenging look. "How'd you get your mom to let you skip dance class to join our theater?"

I frowned at my sister. "Susan! That was rude."

"No, it wasn't," said Susan. "Everybody knows Mackenzie is going to be a professional ballerina. She dances every single day, and last year Mrs. Fleisch wouldn't let her take horseback riding lessons because it would have taken too much time away from her dancing. So I was just wondering."

Mackenzie's smile faltered for only half a second, and then she was grinning again. "It's fine, Anya," she said. "Susan's absolutely right. I had to practically beg my mother to let me do this, but she finally said it would be okay."

I noticed that Austin was staring at Mackenzie's feet, which she'd shifted as she spoke; they were now planted heel-to-heel on the brick walkway, her toes pointing in opposite directions.

Five more actors arrived, four of whom lived right in our neighborhood. Austin directed them to the questionnaires, which were laid out on a rickety table by the clubhouse door. These new arrivals included Mia Kim, who was Susan's best friend and a year behind Austin, Kenzie, and me in school. Mia was probably the most gifted singer in our whole town. Her younger brother, Eddie, was with her; he'd be going into fifth grade next fall. Sam Carpenter was going into sixth grade, like Susan. I didn't know him too well, but he seemed like a sweet kid even though he was kind of shy and had never spoken so much as a single word to me since he'd moved into the neighborhood two years earlier. Maxine Hernandez, who'd been in Susan's class this past year, immediately told us (and made a note on her paperwork) that she was no longer answering to the name Maxine and she preferred to be called Maxie. That was fine with me. I didn't care what she called herself as long as she was willing to bring her trademark style and artistic talent to our hair and makeup department. The fifth person to make his appearance was Deon Becker, Austin's next-door neighbor and tech-savvy best bud.

Deon got dropped off at the curb by his mom, who rolled down the car window and shouted across the clubhouse lawn, "Austin, honey, your mother asked me to remind you to drink plenty of water so you don't dehydrate!"

"Thank you, Mrs. Becker," Austin replied. He nodded politely, but I could tell he was completely embarrassed by his mother's excessive worry, which made me feel a little better about the whole pajama thing.

"We'll set up some chairs," said Austin, giving Deon a nudge toward the cabinet under the stage where they were stored.

Travis Coleman, Elle Tanner, and Gracie Demetrius arrived together in a car pool driven by Gracie's big brother, Nick. They would be in fifth grade next year, so they were a year younger than Susan and the others.

Madeline Walinski and Jane Bailey (who were both going into sixth) showed up next, walking the few blocks from their street. Madeline was chewing bubble gum, which was a habit of hers. I'd ask her to get rid of it before we started. Gum chewing during a rehearsal was the very definition of unprofessional.

Teddy Crawford and Spencer O'Day were last. They were also in Susan's class, which made sense, I suppose, since her Twitter followers were mostly kids her own age. According to Susan, they, along with Maddie and Jane, topped the elementary school A-list. Rumor had it that Spencer was head over heels for Madeline, and Maddie was on the verge of admitting she liked him back.

Teddy was actually a professional actor; he'd had a recurring role on a soap opera when he was a baby, before his family moved here from New York City. He'd also done a macaroni and cheese commercial when he'd been in kindergarten. Having Teddy in our theater would give us what I considered street cred. And Maddie and Jane were both cheerleaders, which meant they could probably rock some pretty complicated dance moves.

Teddy offered to help Austin and Deon set up the folding chairs. Under Austin's direction they arranged thirteen chairs (one for everyone who'd come to audition) facing the stage, just like a real audience.

When everyone had taken a seat, I took a deep breath and made my way to what, in a Broadway theater, would be the orchestra pit. Austin joined me there.

My heart was thudding in my chest like a conga drum.

"Hi, everyone," I said in as confident a voice as I could muster. "Welcome to the first meeting of the Random Farms Kids' Theater. I'm Anya Wallach, and this is my musical director, Austin Weatherly. The purpose of this theater is to put on an extremely cool show."

"Just one?" asked Gracie.

"Well, anything can happen," I conceded, "but for now we're just going to focus on this theatrical revue, giving it all we've got."

Gracie seemed satisfied with my answer. Of course, I was hoping we'd be such a huge success that we'd be able to keep the theater alive for the rest of the summer—and with any luck, our second show would be Austin's original musical. But even hoping for that would be getting ahead of myself, so I just went on talking.

"The revue will be a one-hour performance with singing, dance numbers, and dramatic scenes and skits. Austin, our in-house playwright, has compiled a script that will allow us to work in lots of different kinds of talents."

I paused when the door swung open.

Every head turned to see the silhouette of a girl standing in the sunlight-flooded doorway. She held her pose for a moment as though she were expecting a round of applause. Then she stepped out of the glare, and I saw who it was.

I should have known. Who else but Sophia Ciancio would consider the sun her own personal spotlight?

CHAPTER

"You're late," said Susan.

"Am I?" Sophia looked utterly unapologetic as she glided across the old wooden planks of the floor.

I forced myself not to make eye contact, and continued, "My goal for this summer is not only to put on a totally entertaining show, but also to have some major fun. Today, as you know, we're going to hold auditions."

At this, a few kids squirmed in their seats. Some looked worried.

I knew that look; it was exactly how I'd looked on the day of soccer tryouts.

Out of the corner of my eye, I noticed Susan turn away. I guess she didn't want to see the disappointment on the actors' faces when I told them some of them weren't going to get to stick around long enough to join in on that major fun.

And suddenly I knew I didn't want to see it either.

These kids had come here with big dreams. They wanted to be in a show . . . *my* show . . . and it occurred to me that there was no reason why every single one of them shouldn't get that chance.

I was the director, after all. I made the rules. And rule number one (which I made up on the spot) was that everyone in this room would be part of the cast. I would keep all of them.

I felt the smile spread across my face.

"In this case," I explained, "you're not auditioning *to be in the show* because you already *are* in the show."

I snuck a glance and saw that both Austin and Susan were smiling.

Sophia let out a snort. "That's *so* parks and rec."

I ignored her.

"I don't get it," said Sam. "If we're all automatically in the show, why do we have to audition?"

"Because we have to decide which roles are right for which actors. Once we see what everyone can do, Austin and I will cast you in the most appropriate parts."

"What if we don't like the parts you give us?" asked Madeline.

"That's show biz, kid." Teddy laughed. "You take what you

get, and you like it."

I was glad he'd said it so I didn't have to. The last thing I needed was a bunch of cranky kids complaining about their parts.

"We'll do our best to make everyone happy," Austin promised. "But remember, there are no small parts, only small actors."

I smiled at his use of that old theater adage, which just happened to be absolutely true.

"What Austin means is that every part is important," I clarified. "Even the smaller roles matter, and it's up to the actors to be big enough to make the most of them."

Maxie raised her hand. "I signed up for costumes and makeup," she reminded me. "What am I supposed to do during auditions?"

Austin held up a copy of the script and smiled. "You can look this over and start getting ideas for wardrobe possibilities. You can also sit in on some of the auditions. That'll definitely inspire you." He pointed to Deon. "As our tech specialist, D, you should take a look at the script as well. Maybe start jotting down notes for lighting cues."

"Okay," said Deon. "But . . . what's a lighting cue?"

Austin and I exchanged glances. Deon was an electrical genius and a tinkerer of the first order, but apparently, he would need to be taught how to apply these skills to a theater setting.

"I'll explain it all later," said Austin with a sigh.

"Susan," I said, "will you please hand out the sides?"

Susan nodded and hopped to it. And before anyone could ask, Austin said, "*Sides* is just another word for the scenes you're expected to perform in an audition."

"You'll see we have two options," I explained. "A monologue and a scene. A monologue is kind of like a spoken solo. A scene is dialogue done with a partner."

At the word *partner*, all eyes turned to Teddy, the one professional among us. I could tell everyone was remembering his groundbreaking work in that mac and cheese ad and, of course, they all wanted him for a partner. Teddy was talented enough to make anyone look good.

I could tell that Austin was seeing exactly what I was seeing. We were both relieved when, of the two pages Susan was offering, Teddy took the monologue. Still, I'd been assigned enough group projects in school to know that the process of choosing partners could get pretty hairy. In school it usually turned out to be a popularity contest. I didn't want that to happen in our theater.

"For the partner work," I said quickly, "we'll put names in a hat and draw at random. It's the fairest way to do it."

"Excellent idea," said Austin. "Anyone who wants to do a monologue, raise your hand."

Teddy, Spencer, Mackenzie, and Madeline shot their hands into the air. That left Mia, Sam, Eddie, Gracie, Travis, Elle, Jane, and Sophia.

Sophia . . . who was giving me a very smug look.

"Anya . . . ," she said, standing and motioning for me to follow her. "A word?"

I hated the thought of responding to her command, but since I knew our presence in this clubhouse had everything to do with her, I followed her to the front door. I was happy when Austin joined us.

"What's up?" I asked, trying to sound calm and offhanded.

"You know I have no intention of auditioning, right?"

"What do you mean?" said Austin. "Everyone has to audition. How else will we get a feel for what kind of talent and ability we're working with?"

Sophia gave me an icy smile. "Oh, I think Anya is more than up to speed when it comes to my talent and ability."

"Well, I know you can sneeze on cue," I muttered. "If that's what you mean."

"I mean, I'm easily the best performer in this troupe, and I don't see any need to prove it to you. We made a deal, remember? I got you this quaint little venue. Now I'm calling in the favor."

"The deal was you'd get a role in the revue," I reminded her. "That's it. We never said you didn't have to audition for a part."

Sophia laughed. "OMG, Anya. I mean, come on. What other sort of part would I want? I assumed 'starring role' was implied."

I was about to tell her it wasn't, not at all, and that if she wanted to be a part of Random Farms, she would have to stand up and sing for us like everyone else. But just as I was about to open my mouth, Austin piped up.

"That's fine, Sophia," he said evenly. "We know what you're capable of. We'll cast you in a suitable role."

"And by suitable," Sophia crooned, giving him a flirty smile, "you mean big, right?"

Austin hesitated. Then, to my shock, he nodded. "Okay, Sophia."

I actually felt my hands curling into fists. "Austin . . ."

"Excellent!" Sophia's eyes were shining triumphantly. "So, I guess I'll be on my way. Daria Benson's having some people over for a pool party. I'm one of only three rising seventh graders who got the invite."

"Congratulations," I said through gritted teeth. Then I got a sinking feeling in my belly and asked before I could stop myself, "Who were the other ones?"

"One was your friend Becky," Sophia reported. "But she sent her regrets. Something about having to catch butterflies, I think. I'm not sure who the third person was, but I'm sure it was someone with major status."

I was speechless. Becky had been invited to Daria's party. And she hadn't told me. She'd texted me about her swim meet and the one-hundred-meter butterfly, but Daria's name had never even come up.

I had no idea how to feel about that, so I pushed the thought out of my head and gave Sophia a smile (which I was sure looked more like a snarl). "Have fun," I said. "Be back here tomorrow for rehearsal."

Her expression told me she'd show up whenever she was good and ready. Then she gave Austin a bright smile and flounced out of the clubhouse.

I whirled to face him. "Seriously?"

"What?"

"You promised her a big part without even making her audition for it."

He motioned around at the vast space of the clubhouse. "We wouldn't be here if it weren't for her. What if she ran back to her father and told him to change his mind about this place?"

"He wouldn't do that!" But the truth was I didn't know Dr. Ciancio well enough to say what he would or wouldn't do in that situation. Maybe the thought of Sophia whining and pouting all summer would be enough to make him go back on his word. So Austin had a good point, but still . . . he had no right to make that decision without asking me. If he'd given me a chance, maybe I could have talked Sophia into auditioning. I told him this in a curt tone.

"She wouldn't have agreed to hang around that long," he said. "Daria's party starts at eleven thirty."

I was about to ask him how he knew that when Susan came bounding over.

"Let's get moving," she said. "The thespians are getting restless."

"Where were we?" I asked with a heavy sigh.

"Pairing up for scenes," Austin reminded me. "But with Sophia gone, we're left with an odd number of actors."

Great. An odd number wasn't going to work for partnering.

Reluctantly, I found myself turning to Austin. I was still a little miffed over his giving in to Sophia, but sulking about it wouldn't get us anywhere. "Do you mind . . . ?" I began lamely.

"I'll be the wild card," he said, grabbing an extra questionnaire, tearing off a corner, and writing his name on it.

Sam offered his baseball cap to use for the drawing.

As we shook up the names, Mia asked, "What about the singing auditions?"

"We've chosen a few songs," I said. "You can pick whichever one best fits your voice."

"Mia can sing anything," said Eddie.

I smiled at him. "It's nice that you're so proud and supportive of your big sister."

"I'm not being proud *or* supportive," said Eddie with a roll of his eyes. "I just wanted to say it before she did."

"Well, it's true," said Mia in a matter-of-fact tone. "I'm not bragging, honest. I'm just saying it doesn't matter which song I sing, which might make things easier."

"Thanks, Mia," I said. "It's good to know you're flexible."

"But I guess I am *sorta* proud," Eddie mumbled.

Austin tore seven more little paper rectangles. The actors quickly scribbled their names on these and dropped them into the hat.

"Okay," I said. "I'll draw out two names at a time, and those people will be partners for the audition scene."

This was fine with everybody. I reached into the hat and grabbed two scraps of paper. "Mia and Travis," I announced.

Travis gave Mia a shy smile. Mia beamed.

I dipped into the cap again. "Sam and Eddie."

"Let me pick this time," said Susan. She made a grand gesture of reaching into the hat and drew out two more names with a flourish. "Gracie and Jane."

The girls high-fived each other.

The last two names were Elle and Austin. When I read them aloud, Elle blushed. But to her credit, she didn't flip out or panic or faint. I had a feeling we wouldn't be having any stage fright issues with Elle.

"Wait a minute," said Eddie, looking up from the sides. "This scene is for a boy and a girl."

I shrugged. "So?"

"So . . . my partner is Sam. He's a boy."

Sam laughed. "Thank you, Captain Obvious, for pointing that out."

But I saw the problem now. One of these boys was going to have to play a girl, and something told me Eddie wasn't going to be open to it.

"We've got the same problem," said Gracie, pointing to her partner, Jane. "Should we switch with Eddie and Sam?"

"We could," I said, knowing in my heart it would be the simplest way to go. "But then again, this is all about acting."

"Right," said Austin. "Did you know that in Shakespeare's time, all the female roles were played by men or boys?"

"Why?" asked Mackenzie.

"Because it was against the law for women to be onstage."

"That's ridiculous," said Madeline. "Hadn't they ever heard of equal rights?"

Austin laughed. "Actually, no."

"So, if it was good enough for Mr. Shakespeare," I said, "it should be good enough for us!" I looked from Eddie to Sam, then back to Eddie. "How about one of you plays the opposite gender, just for the audition?"

"What?" cried Eddie. "You're kidding, right? I don't want to play a girl!"

"And I don't want to play a boy," added Jane.

"What's the big deal?" said Gracie. "Like Anya said, it's acting. It might be fun to try playing a boy."

"I bet I could be hilarious as a girl," said Sam, warming to the idea. He batted his eyelashes and patted his hair. "Oh no," he trilled in a falsetto voice. "I think I broke a nail."

"That's insulting!" said Madeline, planting her hands on her hips. "Not all girls are like that."

"Hey, dude!" Gracie said with a rasp, deepening her voice to a hoarse croak. "Check out my muscles! I'm such a tough guy! Anybody got some beef jerky?"

"Not all boys are like *that*," said Teddy. "I hate beef jerky. Although"—he grinned and flexed his biceps—"I do kind of have the muscle thing going on."

"Who wants to go to the mall?" sang Sam in his high voice.

"Cut that out!" snapped Jane.

As the bickering continued, I felt myself losing control of the situation.

"Do something," said Susan. "Before we have a theatrical mutiny on our hands."

She was right. I was the director. It was my job to fix this, but how? The girls were insulted, the boys were getting snarky . . . and none of it had anything to do with acting.

"Everybody, just relax!" I shouted over the escalating quarrel.

I gave them a minute to simmer down. When I had their attention again, I said calmly, "I agree that not all girls are into manicures and not all boys are muscle heads. But this actually brings up an important point about acting technique. Ya see, if Sam decides that his *character* is the kind of girl who cries over chipped nail polish, then that's a valid acting choice. And if Gracie's boy character is a gym rat who likes to gnaw on artificial beef snacks, then that's okay too. Granted, these may not be the most original choices, but it is exactly how an actor brings life to a character. It's called backstory."

This backstory stuff was something I'd overheard some

of the professional actors discussing once during my *Annie* experience. It was a cool feeling to be able to put to good use something I'd learned by actually taking part in a production.

As I let the information sink in, Austin turned and threw me a wink. "I think you just gave them an acting lesson," he said. "Very directorial of you."

"Thanks," I said, realizing he was right. I felt a glimmer of pride.

And suddenly I wasn't so mad about the Sophia thing anymore.

We gave the actors forty-five minutes to rehearse, then got down to business with the acting auditions. Austin and Elle were the first scene partners to read. Sitting in the last row of folding chairs, I felt a flutter of disbelief as I watched them take the stage. *This was happening!*

It was hard not to giggle, thinking of Austin as Peter Pan, because I just couldn't picture him in green tights! But Elle was charming as Wendy. My only real concern was that she kept forgetting to "cheat out" to the audience. I made a note on my legal pad to remind her to angle herself slightly when speaking to another actor so she'd always be facing effectively downstage, or toward the audience, and not turning her profile to them.

After Elle's audition, I (with Susan's help) continued to audition the scene partners on the stage, while Austin took the monologues outside to read on the lawn.

Not surprisingly, Sam's audition was hilarious. His acting choice was to take his Wendy totally over the top, making her more of a caricature than a character, which worked beautifully. I laughed so hard, I almost cried. Eddie was terrific too, keeping up with Sam's energy and never so much as cracking a smile, no matter how wacky Sam got.

Gracie, on the other hand, went a different way entirely with her gender-bending experiment. Despite the silly "boy impersonation" she'd done earlier, for the actual audition she chose to play it with perfect authenticity, digging deep and "becoming" Peter Pan. Susan and I were blown away; Gracie had actually "acted herself" into a boy.

"We've got some real talent here, don't we?" Susan whispered.

"Yes." I nodded, feeling that familiar swirl of excitement in my belly. "We really do!"

Mia and Travis had just finished their scene when Austin and the others returned from outside.

I gave Austin a questioning look to which he responded with a grin and a nod. I took this to mean that he was pleased with what he'd seen during the monologues.

It was time to move on to the dance auditions. Austin dug the sheet music from *How to Succeed* out of my backpack and sat down at the piano.

He played the first few bars and winced. "This baby is way out of tune," he said. "It'll do for now, but we're going to have to get it taken care of before the show."

I told Susan to make a note of that, then I wrangled everyone onto the floor, away from the chairs. "Everybody ready to dance?"

Elle wanted to know if we were going to be doing the fox trot or maybe the tango, both of which she'd taught herself by binge-watching *Dancing with the Stars* episodes on YouTube.

"Sorry, Elle," I said. "No fox trots."

Mackenzie was a little worried about dancing in sneakers as opposed to her actual jazz shoes (or toe shoes or tap shoes or whatever she usually wore for this sort of thing), but thankfully, she didn't make a big deal about it.

Spencer, Eddie, and Gracie just flat out refused to dance at all.

"You can't refuse," I said reasonably. "It's part of the audition process. It's mandatory."

"But I stink at dancing," said Spencer.

"So do I," said Gracie. "I'm what you might call … clumsy." As if to prove it, she accidently backed into the wobbly old table and nearly knocked over my laptop. Fortunately, baseball star Sam was there to catch it before it hit the floor.

"I feel goofy when I dance," Eddie admitted. "It feels like everyone will be looking at me."

"Everyone *will* be looking at you," said Susan. "That's kind of the whole point."

"Look, guys," I said, sighing. "I totally understand. It's exactly how I feel about soccer. But can you at least give it a try? You three can stand in back so you have someone in front of you to follow." I gave them my most hopeful smile. "Hey, you might even like it!"

Spencer, Gracie, and Eddie exchanged looks.

"Fine," said Gracie. "We'll give it a shot. But if I break anything, it's your fault."

We lined everyone up, and Susan and I walked the cast through the combination:

Heel, heel, heel, twist, twist . . . and turn, heel, heel, heel . . . twist, twist, arms!

After several walk-throughs, we added the music. Austin played slowly at first, then picked up the tempo as the kids improved. Mackenzie, of course, had no trouble at all. She didn't just dance, she practically *floated*, which dazzled me and made me jealous at the same time. I let the boys go alone while the girls watched, then switched it up and let the boys watch the girls dance.

"Excellent!" cried Susan. "Gracie, you're doing great."

When the girls were done, I had them all move onto the stage to perform together again, counting them in with an enthusiastic, "Five, six, seven, eight."

Turn . . . heel, heel, heel . . .

I couldn't believe it—they were fabulous! Heads were high, shoulders were back, feet were moving in time with the music. This time they didn't just dance. . . . They performed! I couldn't believe the energy . . . the charisma, the syncopation. Sure, there was a misstep here and there, and a couple of them were a bit stiff, but overall I was blown away.

"Look at 'em go," Susan whispered, her eyes wide, her face beaming.

I made all kinds of notes on my legal pad: *Jane has great facial expressions; Teddy should be positioned toward the back because he's so much taller than the others; Elle has to remember not to stick out her tongue during the box step.*

Even Eddie, Gracie, and Spencer (despite their reluctance) were giving it their all. I was glad I had encouraged them to step outside of their comfort zones.

Make that step-*ball-change* outside of their comfort zones.

When Austin finished the song, Susan and I burst into applause. My dancers were huffing and puffing but smiling. Honestly, I had chills.

"You were fabulous!" I gushed. "Really great. I'm so

impressed by how much you learned so quickly."

"Even me?" Eddie said with a gasp.

"Even you!" I said, laughing, then nodded at Spencer and Gracie. "You guys too!"

I told them to take a few minutes to rest while I made a few more notes. I wrote on my legal pad that in addition to Mackenzie, Travis could probably handle a featured part in the ensemble number.

"What's next?" asked Teddy.

"Singing auditions," Susan announced, hurrying over to the table to grab the music we'd arranged there. There were five songs from which the singers could choose:

"Consider Yourself" from *Oliver!*

"Maybe" from *Annie*

"The Kite" from *You're a Good Man, Charlie Brown*

"Happiness" also from *Charlie Brown*

"Good Morning Baltimore" from *Hairspray*

"I suggest you choose a song you're familiar with," I said. "If you don't know any of these songs, Austin will be happy to work with you."

Mia's hand shot up. "What about a vocal warm-up?"

"Oh. Right." I felt a little silly for not thinking of that myself. I knew it was important for singers to exercise their vocal chords, but since I'd never taken any formal voice lessons myself, I wasn't sure how the exercises were done. "Would you mind leading the cast in the warm-up, Mia?"

Mia said she wouldn't mind at all, which freed me up to consult with my tech crew. I found Deon and Maxie emerging from their exploration of the backstage area.

"How's it going with you two?" I asked.

"Pretty well," said Deon, pointing to the ceiling above the stage. "There's no spotlight, but there are a couple of overhead canister lights with dimmers. That means we can go from total darkness to full brightness."

"No footlights, though," I grumbled, eyeing the stage. Too bad. I'd always liked the idea of footlights. They just felt so theater-y.

"Well . . ." Deon shrugged. "Maybe I can staple-gun a strand of white holiday lights to the front edge of the stage."

"Perfect!" I said, picturing it. "What about microphones and stuff?"

"Well, there are plenty of outlets where we can plug in the sound equipment."

"Wow!" I said. "So you have sound equipment?"

Deon frowned. "No. Don't you?"

"I was hoping we could use the PA system that's already here," I explained.

"We could," D reported. "But it's pretty ancient. I'd probably have to fiddle with it a bit. I did find a couple of wireless handheld microphones, and there's one that hangs from the ceiling."

"That's called an area mic," I said, remembering the term from my *Annie* experience. "It'll amplify voices a little bit, but only if you're standing right beneath it."

I had a sudden unpleasant vision of all my performers huddled together in the middle of the stage, elbowing one another out of the way in a desperate attempt to have their individual voices heard. Not a pretty picture.

Flummoxed, I turned to Austin, who was at the piano, trying to help Madeline choose the song that best suited her vocal range. "Austin, what are your thoughts on the sound situation?"

"The sound situation?"

I motioned for Deon to explain.

When he'd heard the options, Austin took a minute to consider the problem. "I think maybe we should just skip the PA entirely," he decided. "Handheld mics can create feedback. And if we amplify the singer but not the piano, it'll be really hard for the audience to hear the music."

"So no sound at all?"

He grinned. "Just the kind the actors can make on their own."

"In other words, 'sing out, Louise'?"

Austin laughed at my *Gypsy* reference. "Exactly, Mama Rose."

I turned back to D, who looked disappointed. "Maybe next time," I told him. If he only knew how much I was hoping for a next time.

"Let's hear from our wardrobe mistress," I said, smiling at Maxie. "Now that you've read the script, do you have any ideas for costumes?"

"Lots," said Maxie. "I see black leggings with sequins for the dance number. Tons and tons of sequins. Multicolored. And wigs! You've got wigs, right?"

Sure. I keep them with my sound equipment.

No spotlights, no microphones. And where was I going to get tons and tons of sequins on our all-but-nonexistent budget?

"Make a list of everything you're going to need," I advised, handing my pad and pen to Maxie. "Wigs, Christmas lights . . . all of it." Then I patted them each on the shoulder. "And keep up the good work."

Sighing, I went to join Austin at the keyboard. It was time to hear what kind of vocal talent we had.

"Okay, everyone," I said, waving them over. "We're going to begin the singing auditions. Please hold your applause until everyone's had their chances. Now . . . let's do this!"

✧✦✩✧

Mia and Sam were every bit as amazing as I'd expected them to be, maybe even better. Mia sounded like a young version of Idina Menzel, the actress who originated the role of Elphaba in *Wicked*. And Madeline, Teddy, Gracie, Eddie, and Spencer surprised us with their strong voices. Mackenzie and Elle were a little bumpy but not awful.

Then there were Jane and Travis . . .

Yikes!

Yikes wasn't *my* word; it was Susan's. Unfortunately, she made the mistake of saying it out loud.

Travis was only a few bars into his song, "Happiness," when Susan gasped and blurted out the *y* word.

Travis stopped singing abruptly. Everyone froze, wide-eyed . . . especially me.

I knew Susan hadn't meant to be rude; she just couldn't help herself. Travis really was *that* bad. Still, *yikes* didn't exactly fall under the heading of "constructive criticism."

As soon as she realized what she'd done, Susan's face crumpled into an expression of absolute regret. "Oh, Travis! I'm so sorry! I didn't mean to say that. Honest! It just kind of slipped out."

To my shock, Travis didn't seem in the least bit bothered by Susan's outburst. In fact, he laughed. "I know I'm not a singer," he said, with a careless shrug. "I can't carry a tune to save my life. Nobody in my whole family can. We think it's a DNA thing."

Austin cocked his head. "You're okay with that?"

"Sure," said Travis. "I'm only singing now because I thought it was a mandatory part of the audition process. Like the dance lesson."

"Well," I said, "technically, it is. And I appreciate you giving it your best shot."

"I know my singing needs work," said Travis with a laugh. "But I more than made up for it in the dance auditions, didn't I?"

"You did," I agreed. And it was true. After Mackenzie, Travis might have been the best dancer we had.

"Who's next?" said Austin.

"Me," said Jane, hurrying across the floor to stand beside the keyboard.

"Which song will you be singing for us?" I asked.

Jane gave me a confident smile. " 'Maybe.' From *Annie*."

One of my favorites. I settled back in my folding chair and listened as Austin played the intro. Jane pushed back her shoulders, lifted her chin, and began to sing.

Uh-oh.

What had Travis said about his singing difficulties running in the family? I found myself wondering if perhaps he and Jane were distant cousins.

I snuck a look at Susan, who was, for once in her life, speechless. And I knew why. This went way beyond *yikes.*

Then I caught Austin's eye; he looked as uncomfortable as I felt. I allowed myself to glance at the rest of my actors. It was clear that Mia and Sam knew Jane was off-pitch. Even Travis, who was basically tone-deaf, knew Jane was off-pitch.

In fact, it seemed that the only person who didn't know how unbelievably off-pitch Jane was . . .

Was Jane!

Because she was belting out those lyrics and smiling as though she'd already won the Tony award.

"Maaaaaaay-bEEEEeeeeeee!" she finished, her arms outstretched and her eyes shining.

Silence.

Then I guess Mia remembered what I'd said about holding the applause till the end because she began to clap. As the others joined in, Jane thanked Austin and came over to where I was seated.

She beamed at me. I managed a smile.

"So?" Jane was practically glowing with pride. "Do you think I'll be able to sing 'Maybe' in the revue? Do you think I have a shot at doing a solo?"

"Um . . . well . . . " I gulped again and said the only word that came to mind: "*Maybe.*"

CHAPTER

Once again I stood in front of my actors in their folding chairs, Austin by my side.

"I just want to say," I began, "how happy I am that all of you have decided to be part of Random Farms. Now that I know what you can do, I'm more certain than ever that we're going to put on an awesome show."

I nodded for Austin to take over.

"Anya and I are going to cast the show and post the list on that bulletin board over there." He pointed to a corkboard near the entrance. "So please be here tomorrow morning at ten o'clock, ready to learn your parts."

Susan reminded everyone to bring their dues money— ten dollars each—and suggested they pack a lunch and a water bottle as well. I was glad she'd thought of this; nourishment hadn't even crossed my mind.

As everyone got up and shuffled toward the door, Susan let out a heavy sigh and grabbed the broom.

"What's that for?" asked Travis.

"This place isn't going to clean itself," said Susan. "We promised Mr. Healy we'd tidy it up—inside and out—in exchange for letting us use it as our theater."

"Oh," said Mia. "Well, I've got nothing to do for the rest of the day. I can help."

"So can I," said Teddy. "I'm great at yard work."

"I'll dust," Maddie offered. "But I don't do windows."

"I'll do the windows," said Jane.

The next thing I knew, my cast was hard at work inside and outside of the clubhouse. I was thrilled because it had never even occurred to me to ask them, let alone that they would offer! This seemed like a good sign. They were already taking pride in this endeavor. Deon said he should leave to go find our footlights, and Sam apologized profusely for having to head home to work on his curveball. Still, we had all the help we needed, and that freed up me and Austin to work on the casting.

"Thanks, guys," I said. "It would have taken Austin and Susan and I forever to do this ourselves."

"We know," said Teddy with a big grin. "But now you can get right to casting the show. And the faster you do that, the faster we find out what parts we're getting!"

"We should do this in private," I suggested. I didn't want anyone to know what parts they were being considered for until we'd finalized our decisions.

I led Austin outside (where Teddy was already making tremendous progress with the dandelions), and we took a seat under the tall oak tree. He was holding the script; I had my legal pad.

"First things first," said Austin, flipping the pages of *Random Acts of Broadway* with a practiced eye. "I'm going to have to add a few scenes to accommodate everyone, since, ya know, you decided we were keeping them all."

I frowned slightly. "Is that a problem?" I asked.

"No, not really." He held out his hand for my pen. "I just wish you had given me a clue that you were planning to do that."

"I would have," I said, sounding more defensive than I'd meant to. "But I didn't have a clue myself until it happened."

I watched as he made a few notations on the script. "We can use the dance they learned at auditions," he said. "Mackenzie can help take it up a few notches. And I think if we add these acting roles, there'll be a part for everybody."

He showed me the script, where he'd written in the titles of four new numbers:

Scene from WICKED

"Brotherhood of Man" from HOW TO SUCCEED IN BUSINESS WITHOUT REALLY TRYING (Dance number)

Scene from OLIVER!

Monologue from WILLY WONKA AND THE CHOCOLATE FACTORY

"Speaking of 'a part for everybody . . . ,' " I said. "What was that all about with Sophia?"

"What do you mean?"

"You promised her a lead."

"Technically," he said, leaning back against the tree trunk, "*you* promised her a lead."

"I did not!"

He laughed. "Oh, c'mon. This is Sophia we're talking about. You promised her she could be in the show. We should have read between the lines and known she would demand something big. Did you really think she'd be okay with some little background role?"

I scowled. "Okay, first of all, in my theater, background roles are not going to be considered little. I know some people think actors who don't have lines or solos are less important somehow, but did you see how much talent we have? I think we should do everything we can to make even the smallest roles stand out. Then no one ever has to feel like a . . . a . . ."

"A chorus orphan?"

I gasped, because that sounded an awful lot like an insult. "What's that supposed to mean?"

"Nothing," said Austin. "I'm sure you were an awesome chorus orphan."

"Okay, just to be clear, I worked really hard at it."

Austin shook his head. "I'm not saying you didn't. But there are leads, and there are supporting characters, and then there are the ensemble members. It's a hierarchy. Plays are stories, and stories can't be about *everybody*."

Did he think I was an idiot? I *knew* that. Of course I knew that! But as I'd watched all those kids working so hard and doing so well, it had occurred to me that maybe in this theater, we could do things differently. Maybe we wouldn't have to divide actors into "stars" and "background" in a way that was so black-and-white. I had loved every minute of my role in *Annie*. I'd done my best and I knew I'd made an impression. Okay, fine, so maybe Rooster and FDR had had the chance to make a bigger impression, but that didn't take anything away from me. Stars couldn't *be* stars without a cast full of supporting characters. In fact, one of the things

I'd learned was that it was often more difficult for an actor to figure out how to react nonverbally in a scene than it was to deliver dialogue. Or, as the director had put it, "A good actor can respond with lines, but a great actor can react without saying anything at all." That was an important lesson.

I wished I could express this to Austin in a way that would make sense, but he was the one who was so good with words—not me. I would just have to wait and show him what I meant . . . and I couldn't do that until we had our revue up and running.

So I took a deep breath and made myself calm down.

"Fine," I said. "Sophia is a talented girl. It won't hurt the theater to showcase her a little bit." I nodded toward the script. "So what do you have in mind?"

" 'Castle on a Cloud,' " he said immediately.

Well, that was quick! It was as if he'd been thinking about what role to give Sophia since . . . since . . . since the minute he'd seen her in that flouncy little tennis dress! Maybe he'd been thinking about it *because* he'd seen her in that stupid tennis dress.

Eww. I pushed the thought out of my head.

"It's the last big solo in the show, and it's a crowd-pleaser," Austin explained.

Deep down I knew Austin was right. She was perfect for

that song, even if she hadn't had to audition for it.

"We should probably give her a speaking scene too," I said, resigned. "How about the *Wicked* one? If ever anyone was born to play a witch . . ."

Austin laughed. "Done!" He wrote Sophia's name in the two appropriate places. We spent the next hour debating which roles should go to whom. Mostly we agreed, but there were a few parts that tripped us up. For example, I thought Eddie would make an amazing Oliver, but Austin saw him more as Charlie Brown. I wanted the *Fantasticks* dance to be a solo for Mackenzie, but Austin suggested (now that we knew that Travis could dance) we make it a pas de deux—a dance performed by two people.

"I can get on board with that," I said, watching as he added it to the list.

We went on making our casting choices without any more squabbling. Austin was just writing in the last name on the cast list when the clubhouse door swung open and our dusty, dirt-smeared but smiling troupe came out.

"Can we see the list yet?" Travis asked.

I smiled at him. "I'd rather unveil it officially tomorrow morning," I said. Secretly, I wanted a little more time to think about it. Maybe I'd get a great idea for a casting change in the middle of the night.

Eddie frowned, but Mackenzie gave him a friendly elbow to the ribs. "Quit sulking," she said. "The suspense makes it more exciting."

"Thanks, everyone," I called as the Random Farms actors began to disperse. "See you tomorrow. And please don't be late. We have a lot to do. This show goes up in three weeks."

This stopped them in their tracks. Suddenly twelve astonished faces were staring at me. I felt my face turn red. "Uh . . . did I forget to mention that?"

"Yes, you did," said Maddie. "Three weeks?"

"Seriously?" said Teddy.

"We can do it," said Austin in a tone that was both confident and authoritative. "As long as we work hard and focus."

Jane rolled her eyes. "If you say so."

Again, the kids headed on their way.

"I'll e-mail them the rehearsal and performance schedules tonight," Susan promised as she, Austin, and I headed back to our house. "How'd the casting go?"

"Excellent," I said. "I think they'll all be happy with the roles we gave them. How'd the cleanup go?"

"It looks brand-new in there," Susan announced. "Not a dust bunny or a cobweb in sight."

"Better not tell Mom that," I warned.

"Why not?"

"Because if she realizes you actually know how to clean, she's going to expect you to do something about that room of yours!"

Susan gave me a look. Then she burst into "It's the Hard Knock Life" and belted it out all the way home.

⋆✦⋆✧

We arrived in our driveway to see our neighbors' garage door going up and revealing Mr. Quandt dressed in overalls and Mrs. Quandt in an old smock with a scarf tied over her hair.

"Hello, girls," said Mrs. Quandt. "Your mother tells me you've taken on a theater project."

"Not a project," I corrected politely. "An actual theater." I eyed her sloppy clothing, which was so unlike the crisp, tidy manner in which she usually dressed. "What are you up to?"

"Just a long overdue cleanup," she said, picking up a bulging garment bag and dragging it down the driveway. "So much clutter. So little room!"

Austin, a true gentleman, immediately took the bag from Mrs. Quandt. After he'd deposited it at the curb, he hurried back to the garage and offered to help Mr. Quandt lift a heavy table.

"We're simplifying," Mr. Quandt explained. "These things

are still useful, they're just a little too worse for wear, so they're all going to the donation center. Healy should be by any minute to haul everything away in his pickup truck."

I examined the overstuffed garment bag. "What's in here?"

"Oh, just a lot of outdated things. Some old business suits, a couple of prom gowns from when my daughter was young. I think there may even be a few dresses that belonged to my grandmother."

"In the olden days?" asked Susan.

Mrs. Quandt laughed. "Yes, Susan, in the olden days."

I followed her back to the garage where she lovingly ran her hand over an old cabinet-model sewing machine. "I do wish this didn't have to go. It's the machine I learned on. But it hasn't worked in years, and the company no longer makes replacement parts. Besides, I have a brand-new portable model Mr. Quandt bought me for our anniversary."

I had forgotten how much Mrs. Quandt loved to sew. When Susan and I were little, she used to help Mom with our Halloween costumes. And one summer she made us matching terry cloth beach cover-ups.

Austin was now assisting Mr. Quandt in carrying a flow-ered love seat to the curb.

"You know," I said, "I bet those old suits and gowns could come in really handy for costumes. And all this furniture

114

would make terrific set pieces."

"You really want all this old junk?" asked Mr. Quandt, eyeing the worn love seat and battered chairs.

"Not junk," I corrected politely. "Props!" I turned to Mrs. Quandt. "Do you by any chance happen to have any wigs?"

"As a matter of fact..." Mrs. Quandt pointed to a large box.

Susan opened the box and gasped. She pulled out a blond pixie-cut wig, a sleek black one cut into a bob, and a long wavy auburn one. From where I stood, I could see that there were still plenty more in the box—white curls, long sandy tresses, and even a silver one with purple streaks. Susan and I both turned slowly with wide eyes to look at our neighbor.

Mrs. Quandt laughed again. "What can I say, dears? It was the seventies."

"What's in here?" asked Susan, opening an old trunk.

"Just a bunch of mismatched bed linens," said Mrs. Quandt. "Sheets, quilts, pillowcases."

When Mr. Healy pulled up in his truck, Mr. Quandt and Austin began loading things into the back.

"Change of plans, Healy," said Mr. Quandt cheerfully. "We're donating these to Anya's project. These theater types here have agreed to take all this junk off our hands."

"Not junk," I reminded him with a big smile. Then added in a whisper, "Magic!"

RANDOM FARMS THEATER SCHEDULE

WEEK ONE
Monday, June 21–Friday, June 25: 10:00 a.m. to 5:00 p.m.

WEEK TWO
Monday, June 28–Friday, July 2: 10:00 a.m. to 5:00 p.m.

*Monday, July 5: no rehearsal because
of the extended holiday weekend*

HAPPY INDEPENDENCE DAY!

WEEK THREE (TECH WEEK)
Tuesday, July 6–Thursday, July 8: 10:00 a.m. to 5:00 p.m.

DRESS REHEARSAL
Friday, July 9: 10:00 a.m. to AS LONG AS IT TAKES!

OPENING NIGHT

RANDOM ACTS OF BROADWAY
Saturday, July 10: 7:00 p.m.
Call Time: 5:00 p.m. (entire cast and crew)

When I entered the theater the next morning, I had to catch my breath.

Streamers of sunlight filtered in through the sparkling windows. The floors had been scoured and polished until they gleamed. According to Susan, both restrooms had been scrubbed and sanitized by—to my great shock—Eddie Kim, who'd volunteered after everyone else had flat out refused to have anything to do with cleaning the long-untouched "facilities." Eddie had worn rubber gloves and wielded his toilet brush like a pro.

During the cleaning, Susan had discovered a deep storage closet backstage, which she and Maxie had cleared out to create an instant wardrobe department. It was just waiting to welcome all the Quandts' old clothes, hats, and, of course, wigs! When Maxie arrived, I would have her start emptying the boxes and garment bags (which Mr. Healy had left rather unceremoniously in the middle of the stage) and arranging them in the closet.

Behind me, the door opened.

"Good morning, Madam Director," said Austin.

I smiled, momentarily dazzled by a slant of sunshine that flashed off the lenses of his glasses. He was carrying a pile of scripts and songbooks from his own personal collection. He placed these on the Quandts' former kitchen table, which had replaced the old rickety one by the door.

"Mr. Playwright," I said with a formal nod and a little giggle.

We had agreed to meet here early to post the official cast list. I hadn't made any midnight changes to it after all. I realized that my gut instincts (and Austin's) were spot-on, and the choices we'd made were perfect just the way they were.

I opened my backpack, took out the two-page list, and approached the large cork bulletin board that had once held neighborhood notices about bake sales, bridge tournaments, and babysitters needed. Two shiny little thumbtacks remained pushed into the otherwise empty board, which seemed like a very good omen to me. It was as if they'd been waiting there all this time for me to do what I was about to do.

As always, Austin seemed to be reading my mind. "Feels

pretty official, doesn't it?"

I positioned the pages in the center of the corkboard and inserted a thumbtack into the top of each page.

And there it was!

RANDOM ACTS OF BROADWAY CAST LIST

OPENING NUMBER
"Comedy Tonight" from A FUNNY THING HAPPENED
ON THE WAY TO THE FORUM
Full Cast

"Anything You Can Do" from ANNIE GET YOUR GUN
Madeline as Annie Oakley
Teddy as Frank Butler

"Seize the Day" from NEWSIES
Dance solo: Travis
Vocals: Full Cast

Scene from PETER PAN
Jane as Wendy
Spencer as Peter Pan

"Maybe" from ANNIE
Soloist: Mia

Monologue from YOU'RE A GOOD MAN, CHARLIE BROWN
Teddy as Charlie Brown

Scene from WICKED
Sophia as Glinda
Elle as Elphaba

Scene from OLIVER!
Sam as Oliver (soloist: "Where Is Love?")
Eddie as Dodger

Monologue from WILLY WONKA AND
THE CHOCOLATE FACTORY
Gracie as Veruca Salt

"Try to Remember" from THE FANTASTICKS
Dance duet: Mackenzie and Travis

"Castle on a Cloud" from LES MISÉRABLES
Soloist: Sophia

"Brotherhood of Man" from HOW TO SUCCEED
IN BUSINESS WITHOUT REALLY TRYING
Dance: Full Cast

CLOSING NUMBER "There's No Business Like Show Business"
from ANNIE GET YOUR GUN
Full Cast

CURTAIN CALL
Full Cast

"I hope Jane won't be too upset about not singing 'Maybe' in the show," I said.

"She'll be okay," Austin assured me. "And she'll be great as Wendy."

Austin went over and sat down at the piano. He plinked out a few notes, then a few more. Then he added chords. It was a melody I'd never heard before, upbeat and very catchy.

"What is that?" I asked. "It's really good."

Austin smiled and played the notes again. "Oh, it's just something I'm working on," he said. "Just . . . ya know . . . our theme song!"

My eyes went round. "Did you say theme song?"

"Yep!"

"Austin, that is so cool!" I went over and slid beside him on the bench. I'd never even thought of having a theme song, but now I couldn't imagine not having one. "Play it again."

He did. If joy had a sound, this would be it. The notes swirled and bounced and tickled the air of the theater like laughter. The song went straight to my heart.

"Let's hear the lyrics!"

"They aren't finished yet," said Austin. "Still a little rough. But I'm working on them."

I let him play the song through another time. "Austin, we have to use this in the show!"

He beamed. "That's sort of what I was hoping for. I mean, I compiled the script, but there really isn't a lot in it that's mine. I figured this would be the best way for me to put my own stamp on the revue. Like you're doing with your producing and directing. But I don't know if I'll be done in time."

"Sure you will," I said breezily. "Look how fast you put together the revue. And you've got the music nearly completed."

"Yes, but I'm thinking there should be some awesome harmonies, and that'll take a while for the kids to get right. Teaching it to them might take longer than writing."

"It would be amazing if the cast could sing it during the curtain call." I turned to frown at the stage. "Speaking of which . . ."

The ceiling above the stage was equipped with the necessary hardware for a simple proscenium-style stage curtain that could go up and down thanks to some pulleys that dangled in the wings. But there was no actual curtain in place. I supposed we could make do without one, but the thought of seeing a real curtain go up on opening night gave me chills.

Maybe Deon could figure out a way to rig up something. I'd have to work on that.

Austin continued to fiddle with the theme song until

Susan arrived and showed us her design for the program. "We can have the kids write their bios during the lunch break," she suggested.

"Good thinking," I said.

At ten o'clock on the dot the door swung open and all eleven actors rushed in, anxious and excited.

"Where's the list?" asked Madeline.

Austin pointed to the bulletin board; the kids stormed it like a stampeding herd. "Now I know where the term *cattle call* comes from," Austin quipped.

For the next few minutes there were shouts of joy, shrieks of excitement, and high fives and hugs all around. The only person who looked a little unhappy was Jane, but to her credit she didn't sulk, and she was the first to congratulate Mia on getting the solo. I decided I'd have a quiet word with Jane at the end of the day. Exactly what I would say to her, I had no idea. But something told me this was what a real director would do. I hoped Austin would offer to join me for this discussion, but if he didn't, I decided I wouldn't ask. No reason for both of us to be uncomfortable.

Deon and Maxie came in while the cast was still scanning the list. Maxie was holding a large expandable makeup case. Deon was draped with electrical cords and carrying a toolbox.

"Hey," said Mia, "why does Sophia Ciancio get the final solo?"

"Yeah," said Spencer. "She didn't even stick around long enough to sing."

"It's a long story," I said. "But she's very talented, so she'll be a wonderful addition to our cast."

Mackenzie, who knew Sophia as well as I did, looked skeptical. I knew it wasn't the "talented" part she was questioning. . . . It was the "wonderful."

First I had everyone give Susan his or her dues money. It felt weird asking kids for cash, but we had expenses. Programs and tickets would have to be printed, and paper and ink weren't cheap. In addition, Jane had blown through an entire economy-size bottle of my mom's Windex yesterday, which I fully intended to replace.

Once that task was handled, I told everyone to spread out across the floor for some warm-up exercises, and then I stood in front of the group. I was familiar with a few from my rehearsals for *Cinderella* and *Annie*. But last night I'd googled "acting warm-ups" and, with the help of wikiHow and YouTube, I'd added a few more exercises to my repertoire. I invited Mackenzie, possibly the most flexible human being on earth, to help me lead a stretching routine.

We had just begun the first simple stretch when Sophia

strolled in.

"Good morning," she said, dropping her pricey tote bag by the door and looking totally bored with life. "So, where's the cast list?"

Both of my arms were above my head, so I motioned toward the bulletin board with my chin. Sophia examined the list, then turned to me with a smug smile.

"I'm singing 'Castle on a Cloud' and Mia Kim isn't?"

I nodded, gritting my teeth as I reached outward with my left arm, then my right.

"Mia's singing 'Maybe,' " said Jane.

"I can read," snapped Sophia. She turned back to the board. "Oh, and I'm doing a scene from *Wicked* with Elle." She glanced around the room until her eyes fell on her partner. "I hope you know what you're doing," she said. "I refuse to work with amateurs."

"We're all amateurs, Sophia," said Austin firmly. "Well, except for Teddy."

"Teddy's done TV commercials and even had a small role on a soap opera once," said Madeline.

"Well, then I want to do my scene with him," said Sophia, crossing the floor to take a place right at the front of the group.

"Keep stretching," I whispered to Kenzie. "Ignore her."

Kenzie dropped her chin to her chest and began slowly swinging her head from shoulder to shoulder, then in a full circle. "Head rolls," she announced.

"Oh, heads are gonna roll all right," Sophia muttered, "if I don't get to do my scene with Teddy."

It was then that Susan marched right up to Sophia and cleared her throat loudly. "*Ahhhmmm.*"

"What do you want?" sneered Sophia.

"Ten bucks," said Susan, holding out her upturned palm. "Dues money. Everyone paid. Now it's your turn."

Sophia rolled her eyes. "There's money in the outside pocket of my tote. But I only have a twenty."

"No problem," Susan informed her, skipping toward the tote bag. "I can make change. Do you prefer a ten or two fives?"

"Time for some tongue twisters," I said brightly, "to warm up your . . . um . . . well, your tongues, I guess."

A ripple of laughter floated through the theater.

"Really use those cheeks and lips when you say the words," I explained. "Use your whole face and pronounce the words as clearly as you can. Here we go . . . red leather, yellow leather . . . red leather, yellow leather."

Suddenly the whole room was alive with the silly chant. After a minute or so of this I switched to the far more challenging, "I love New York, unique New York, you know you need unique New York." It wasn't long before everyone was giggling.

"What are these for, anyway?" Sam asked.

"They help you focus on enunciating," I told him. "So the words don't run together and the audience can understand you."

"Plus they're fun," said Susan.

I asked Mia to do some voice warm-ups too, since I didn't want to have any strained vocal chords on my conscience.

Once everyone had warmed up, it was time to begin rehearsing in earnest. Deon was anxious to see how the over-head lights would illuminate the stage when everyone was on it, so we started with the dances. The revue now included the ensemble number and one duet—Mackenzie and Travis dancing to "Try to Remember" from *The Fantasticks*, which Austin would play on the piano. Mackenzie would choreo-graph, and I had no doubt it would be breathtaking.

I was pleased with how well everyone had picked up the dance. Sophia caught on quickly enough, which was good because we didn't have to spend any extra time teaching her.

After a few run-throughs, we broke for lunch, during which Susan handed out sheets of paper and had everyone write their bios.

"What's a bio?" asked Sam. "Like our life story?"

"Kind of," I said. "A bio is where you tell the audience a little about yourself, specifically about your previous roles and other theatrical experience."

"What if we don't have any?" asked Jane.

"Just say something like: 'Jane is thrilled to be getting her start here at the Random Farms Kids' Theater.'"

"Ooh!" Jane smiled. "I like that!"

Jane, Mia, Elle, and Madeline finished writing their bios quickly and took the opportunity to pore over a teen magazine Jane had brought along in her backpack. It included a quiz to determine which member of the newest boy band, Dream Four, had the most "boyfriend potential" on a scale of one to ten.

Madeline popped a huge bubble gum bubble and blushingly admitted that even though she had a life-size poster of the group's mischievous lead singer, Dylan Hastings, hanging in her room, she still thought Spencer O'Day had way more BFP than any member of Dream Four.

After the break, everyone split up to rehearse scenes and monologues, just as we had on Saturday, only this time the cast was working on the material they would actually perform in the show. As our actors rehearsed, Austin and I made our way around the theater, spending time with each group or individual, giving them notes and suggestions, and complimenting them on the acting choices that were working.

"I would like everyone to be off book by next Monday," I announced. Then I had to explain to Elle and Eddie what *off book* meant. "Have your lines memorized," I clarified.

"I have a tip," said Teddy. "When I'm preparing for a part, I always tape my pages to the bathroom mirror so I can look at them while I'm brushing my teeth."

"Excellent idea," said Austin.

Maxie was flying around the place with costumes and accessories, handing out hats and slipping on jackets. She asked if any of the girls had character shoes. Some did; I still had my pair from fifth grade somewhere in the back of the closet, and it was bound to fit somebody. Sophia, I was sure, had an extra pair lying around too, but naturally she didn't offer to share.

The actors continued to run their lines, the singers worked on their songs with Austin, and I sat down to look at Maxie's and Deon's sketches for the sets and scenery. They'd done a great job of pulling together Fagin's hideout for Eddie and Spencer's *Oliver!* number. One of Mrs. Quandt's daughter's prom gowns would make the perfect dress for Madeline to wear as Annie Oakley during her "Anything You Can Do" duet with Teddy.

Everything was coming along nicely. The whole theater was humming with activity. Even the out-of-tune piano sounded beautiful to me.

I spent some time at the Quandts' old kitchen table helping Susan write copy for the program and coming up with a design for the tickets. I knew exactly what I wanted them to look like, because I still had the ticket stub from the first Broadway show I'd ever seen saved in a scrapbook.

I tore a sheet of legal paper from my pad and began to write.

"They should look just like this," I said, sliding the page across the tabletop.

The Random Farms Kids' Theater Premiere Performance
THE CLUBHOUSE THEATER
Random Farms Circle, Chappaqua, NY

RANDOM ACTS OF BROADWAY   Row 1 Seat A
7:00 P.M. SUNDAY, JULY 11 $5.00

"Wait," said Susan. "We're charging only five dollars per ticket?"

I nodded.

"That seems kind of cheap. I was thinking we'd charge at least ten. This show is worth it."

"I know," I said. "But this is what Mom would call a marketing strategy. I want to get people in the door— grown-ups *and* kids. When they see how great we are, the grown-ups will be like, 'Wow, I would have paid a lot more to see a show that good,' and the kids will be like, 'I didn't expect it to be so awesome. Where do I sign up for the next show?' "

Susan grinned. "The next show, which will cost ten dollars per ticket. And signing up new actors means more dues money!"

"Exactly," I said. "We're building a reputation, see? We're creating a fan base." I didn't say so out loud, but I knew this was the best shot we had at turning our single musical revue from a one-off into an ongoing theatrical business venture.

"Genius," said Susan, shaking her head in awe. "My sister is an absolute genius!"

"Well, I don't know about *that*," I said, blushing.

"It's the dog-walking business all over again," Susan observed. "Only better."

"Let's hope so," I said, laughing. But she was right. This

wasn't the first time I'd employed my savvy marketing skills and business know-how.

Three years ago I had had the idea to start a dog-walking business in my neighborhood. I'd knocked on the door of every house in our neighborhood where I'd known there was a dog and given my pitch: *dog walking—three dollars for one lap around the cul-de-sac.* Five dollars extra if they'd wanted me to give their pet a bath.

My dad had said I'd had "the entrepreneurial spirit." And I'd made a decent amount of money, too, until Susan had had a major allergic reaction to a Boston terrier I'd been shampooing in our bathtub. That was when Mom had made me retire.

Now I noticed that Susan had taken my pencil and was scribbling something on my ticket mock-up. "What are you doing?"

"You forgot to add the year."

"I think people will get that it's *this* year," I said.

"Duh," said Susan. "Of course they will. But we have to put the year on the ticket anyway!"

"How come?"

"Because," my little sister said with a glowing smile, "someday when Anya Wallach is a big-time world-famous Broadway director, people are going to want to know exactly when it all started."

Her words went right to my heart, filling me with pride. And hope.

CHAPTER

Later, Deon's mom, a former elementary school art teacher, arrived bearing two enormous shopping bags filled to bursting with art supplies. There were two huge rolls of mural paper, several packages of construction paper, tempera paint, and paintbrushes in a range of sizes. . . . The works!

"This stuff has been collecting dust in the attic since I retired," she said. "I thought perhaps you could put it to good use making backdrops and posters."

"Thanks, Mrs. Becker," I said, accepting the coffee can full of magic markers she offered. "This is really generous of you. And I'm sure none of it will go to waste." I was already envisioning a splashy glittery backdrop for Mackenzie's dance solo.

"All right, then." Mrs. Becker smiled and waved to Deon, who was checking a wire. "Let's go, Deon. Dinner isn't going to make itself."

"Dinner?" I looked at my watch. "How did it get to be five o'clock already?"

"Five o'clock?" cried Mackenzie. "I've got a ballet class at five thirty. I've got to go!" She grabbed her things and bolted out the door.

"If anyone's still wearing a costume," Maxie said loudly, "please leave it in the wardrobe department!"

This resulted in a mad rush to the storage closet, with feather boas, crinoline skirts, and cowboy hats flying in every direction.

"Don't forget to take your scripts and sheet music with you," Austin reminded the cast. "We expect you to practice at home."

In a matter of three minutes the entire theater was empty except for me, Austin, and Susan.

And Jane. I had meant to talk to her about "Maybe," but evidently, she was taking matters into her own hands.

"Anya, do you have a second?"

"Sure, Jane."

She didn't beat around the bush. "I was really hoping for a solo."

"I know . . . ," I began. "And I wish I could have given you one. But . . ." I trailed off, unsure of what to say next.

Austin saved me. "It was an artistic decision," he said, which didn't exactly explain the bigger problem of Jane's inability to stay on key, but it sounded good.

"Sophia got a solo and she didn't even audition," Jane reminded us. "Was that an artistic decision too?"

"No, that was a business decision," I said with a sigh.

Jane frowned, but she didn't look angry or even insulted. She looked curious. "I don't understand."

I didn't know how to explain my choice without hurting her feelings. Then I noticed her backpack with the magazine stuffed into the outside pocket, and inspiration struck.

"Okay," I said. "Remember how you and Mia and the others were doing that 'on-a-scale-of-one-to-ten' thing earlier? That quiz to see which Dream Four member would make the best boyfriend?"

"Yeah. What about it?"

"Well, I heard you give Dylan Hastings a five for hairstyle, an eight for dance moves, and a nine-point-two for . . . what was it again?"

Jane's eyes shot to Austin, and her cheeks turned bright pink. "Kissability."

"Right. Then Mia gave his band mate Li'l Q a seven for hair, a three for dance, and a ten for . . . ya' know . . . the kissing thing."

"That's because Li'l Q is a total hottie."

"But when you add up the points, Dylan earns a"—I did some quick mental math—"a twenty-two-point-two, whereas Li'l Q scores only a twenty. So that means even though both of them are big stars in a hot band, according to the quiz, Dylan has the most boyfriend potential."

"I get that," said Jane. "But what's it got to do with my singing audition?"

"If I were going to score you and Mia on the same kind of number scale, I would have given you a ten for enthusiasm. Unfortunately, I would have given you only a five for your ability to match pitch. Mia, on the other hand, would have gotten a ten in both categories."

"Which means Mia was the one with the most solo potential," Austin clarified.

"I know you're disappointed," I said as gently as I could. "But I hope you understand that Austin and I cast the show as we thought best. That doesn't mean it won't happen eventually. Maybe I can ask Mia to help you work on matching pitch."

I wished I could have said, "Maybe you'll get a solo next time," but who knew if there'd even *be* a next time?

"But, Anya," said Jane, with a whine in her voice, "I really wanted to sing 'Maybe.' "

"I get that. But you have to understand how casting works. Lots of actors want parts they don't get. You're going to be an important part of the show, even without a solo. I'm the director, and the director decides."

Jane sighed, folded her arms, and tapped her foot.

"Was there anything else?" I asked.

She looked at me for a long moment. "I guess not," she said a bit saucily.

With that, she turned and left.

"Ugh," I said. "That was awkward."

Austin gave me a sympathetic look. "It's true, you know."

"What's true?"

"You're the director. The director is the boss."

"I've never been good at being bossy," I confessed.

"Being the boss is different than being bossy. Bossy people just like to throw their weight around, but the boss is the person who keeps things going smoothly, the one with the vision, the one who takes charge and shoulders the responsibility."

"Sounds exhausting," I said.

"Oh, it will be," Austin said on a chuckle. "But you can handle it. You just have to remember to stand your ground and stick to your principles and focus on what's best for the show."

I smiled. It felt good to have Austin backing me up this way.

"Let's call it a day," I said, heading for the door.

"I think I'm gonna hang around for a bit," said Austin, glancing toward the piano. "I've got a few more bars of that melody stuck in my brain, and I want to get them down before I lose them."

"Okay," I said, tossing him the key. "Lock up."

As I headed down the front steps, I heard him at the piano playing the catchy tune of our as-yet-unfinished theme song. It really did have a way of getting into your head. In fact, I found myself whistling it the whole way home.

☆☆☆☆

The rest of the week was a blur of scenes, songs, dance routines, and other prep work. I suppose things went as smoothly as they could have, considering we were seventeen kids flying by the seats of our pants. I found myself making new rules as situations arose, like "No throwing baseballs in the theater, Sam" (after a very near miss with a canister light), and "Chewed bubble gum *must* go in the wastebasket, Maddie" (following an unfortunate but hilarious incident with a sticky pink blob and Sophia Ciancio's new designer sandals).

Mostly, though, it was about the theater and the work, about the acting and singing and dancing. I took great pleasure in seeing my cast improve. By Thursday, Eddie barely complained about the dancing anymore, and somewhere during "Seize the Day," Jane actually started singing on pitch. I guess Mia had found some time to work with her. Another happy development was watching as we changed from a bunch of kids who happened to live in the same town to an actual company of actors and, in some cases, friends.

And in one instance . . . significant others.

Which was why rule number three was: "No holding hands during the opening number, Maddie and Spencer."

"Why not?" Spencer asked.

"Well, for one thing, it messes up the dance steps," I told him as patiently as I could. "And for another, it makes Elle and Eddie giggle uncontrollably. So can we possibly hold the romance until after rehearsal?"

Maddie blushed, but Spencer agreed.

Then Austin leaned in close to me and whispered, "Maybe in the next show we should give those two a scene from *Romeo and Juliet.*"

"Maybe," I said, trying not to be flustered by the leaning-in-and-whispering element of the conversation. "Although, I'm pretty sure a balcony would break our budget. And

besides"—I stopped when I realized what he'd just said—
"you really think we're going to do another show?"

"That's the plan, isn't it?"

"Well, yeah, but . . ." I felt my skin tingling with anticipa-
tion. I'd been trying not to think too much beyond this first
performance, since it required every ounce of my focus and
attention. Not to mention, I was afraid of getting my hopes
up. But the way Austin had said it, the way he'd so casually
and confidently referred to our "next show," really made it
feel possible.

On Friday at five o'clock, my parents surprised us by
having six large pizzas delivered to the theater. Dad and Mom
showed up with napkins, paper cups, and soda and joined us
for the impromptu dinner party.

"Anya, the theater is gorgeous," said Mom.

"I don't see a curtain, though," said Dad.

"Working on it," I mumbled around a mouthful of sausage
and mushrooms.

I noticed that Mackenzie had opted not to eat any pizza,
not even a slice.

"Must be a ballerina thing," Austin guessed as we watched
Kenzie offer her pepperoni slice to Maxie, who accepted it
happily.

When dinner was through, I sent the company home,

reminding them to rest their voices over the weekend. In recognition of all my (and Susan's) hard work, Mom and Dad offered to stick around and clear away the paper plates and pizza boxes for us. At first I said no thanks, because the theater was my responsibility after all, which meant the cast's mess was my mess. But Mom insisted, citing the dark circles under my eyes and the fact that Susan couldn't seem to stop yawning.

"Go home and relax," said Dad. "I'm sure even Andrew Lloyd Webber takes a break now and then."

"Okay," I said at last. "Thanks. And don't forget to lock up." I tossed Mom the key, gave them each a hug, and hurried out the door to catch up with Mackenzie, who was heading in the same direction.

"Kenz!" I called. "Wait up." When I reached her, I gave her a big grateful smile. "I just wanted to tell you how much I appreciate all your help with the choreography, and with teaching the less experienced dancers."

"You're totally welcome," she said. "I like teaching. It's been kind of nice being the one not *taking* orders for a change."

"Orders?"

"Oh, well . . . you know what I mean. My dance teachers can be pretty intense. For me, dance is serious business. Like for you theater is business."

"Business," I repeated. "Right. But ballet can also be fun, can't it?"

Mackenzie just smiled and sighed. We started walking again.

"Anyway," I continued, "I just wanted to tell you that we're going to list you as dance captain in the program."

"That's awesome. Thanks."

We walked a little farther, enjoying the early evening quiet that had settled over the neighborhood. But there was a question nagging at the back of my mind, and when we reached the end of her driveway, I blurted it out.

"Don't you like pizza?"

She looked at me strangely. "I love it."

"So . . . why did you give your piece to Maxie?"

Mackenzie's eyes darted quickly to the front door of her house, then back to me. "I like pizza a lot. And cheeseburgers and cupcakes and banana splits . . . but ballerinas tend to stay away from foods like that."

She laughed, although I wasn't sure why. Passing up banana splits didn't seem at all humorous to me. I loved banana splits.

"Don't worry," she said with a wave. "I'm sure there's a big plate of broiled chicken and steamed veggies waiting for me on the kitchen table."

I tried to return her laughter, but I still wasn't sure what was funny.

"See you on Monday, Anya," she said, making her way gracefully up the walk.

"See ya, Kenz," I replied. I almost added, "Enjoy the veggies," but something told me the joke—whatever it had been—was over.

CHAPTER

I woke up on Saturday to a gloomy sky and the sound of rain pattering against my window. I was actually surprised at how bummed I was that we wouldn't be rehearsing today. It had been such a terrific week, and I wished I didn't have to wait until Monday to see Austin and my cast again.

Thunder rumbled overhead. *Noises off*, I thought. Fitting.

I had just thrown my legs over the side of the bed when Susan came bounding into my room.

"Don't you knock?" I said, stuffing my feet into my fluffy pink slippers.

She ignored the question. "I made posters! Cool ones. With the name of the show and the date and time and location."

To prove it, she shoved a sheet of paper at me—it was the 8 1/2 by 14 kind my dad called "legal-size."

"I hope you asked Dad if you could use his work stuff," I said before eyeing the fabulously colorful flyer she'd printed out.

"We can pay him back," she said, flopping beside me on the bed. "Out of the ticket money. Like the Windex." She tapped the flyer. "Just look at that!"

I felt myself grinning as a flash of lightning illuminated the room. "These are actually great," I said. "Seriously! I love the font you picked, and the colors are perfect. We can post them in all the shops in town and at the pool and the tennis courts. And the coffeehouse! We should start hanging them up today!"

"Correction," said Susan. "*You* should start hanging them. I'm going to the movies with Mia and Elle." She beamed, looking very pleased with herself. "Mom's dropping us off, and Elle's dad is picking us up. Rumor has it Maddie and Spencer are going too. We're going to spy on them to see if they kiss!"

I laughed. "Don't do that," I advised.

As much as I would have liked her company (not to mention her help) on my poster-hanging errand, I didn't have the heart to ask her to cancel her movie plans on my account. Especially since I knew this would be Susan's first official cinema excursion without parents. It was practically a rite of passage.

"I've already swiped Dad's stapler and a couple of rolls of Scotch tape," she informed me.

"Swiped?"

"Okay, borrowed. Mom said it would be okay to hang the posters as long as you asked the store owners for permission. So you don't end up in jail."

I was about to tell Susan I was pretty sure they didn't throw kids in jail for putting up posters when my phone pinged, indicating a text message.

My heart leaped a bit, thinking it might be from Austin. It wasn't, but I was not at all disappointed to see who had sent it.

Becky!

Swimming canceled cuz of rain. Let's hang out!!!

I immediately texted her back: **Awesome! I'm going into town to hang posters. Wanna help?**

Becky's response: **Totally! Will bring umbrella. Be over in 15.**

I was dressed and waiting on the front porch in ten. I couldn't wait to tell her—in person—how the first week of rehearsals had gone. We'd been texting and even managed to fit in a Skype session or two, but it just wasn't the same as telling her about it face-to-face.

I decided to take along the money we'd collected as dues—one hundred and thirty dollars total, all in tens and fives. This would be a good opportunity to stop at the bank and exchange it for singles, which we would need for making change when tickets went on sale. I put the wad of bills carefully into the inside pocket of my rain jacket and zipped it closed. I had never carried so much money on me at one time, and frankly, it made me a little nervous.

Soon enough Becky came splashing up our front walk in her pink paisley rain boots, holding what I assumed was a golf umbrella. The thing was huge. It was practically a tent!

Which was why she hadn't felt the need to wear her rain jacket.

Which was why I could see that she had on a brand-new T-shirt:

PROPERTY OF
CHAPPAQUA MIDDLE SCHOOL
GIRLS' SOCCER

"C'mon!" she cried, laughing and waving for me to join her under the umbrella.

I wish I could say the sight of that shirt didn't bother me at all. I wish I could say, now that I had the theater up and running, I didn't care one little smidge about Becky being part of the team and getting invited to Daria Benson's house for pool parties.

I wished I could.

But I couldn't. Not completely, anyway. It wasn't that I didn't feel thrilled about Random Farms and the show and my amazing cast, but in spite of all that, something inside me still twisted a bit at the sight of that shirt. It made me feel apart from Becky somehow . . . disconnected . . . even if we were about to be scrunched up against each other under her big umbrella.

It was almost like landing face first on the soccer field all over again.

But I shook it off, like the raindrops trickling off the nylon of her umbrella. I was hanging with my best friend for the first time in a week, and I refused to let something as silly as a team T-shirt ruin it.

So I took a deep breath and tucked the posters, tape, and stapler under my rain jacket, and we headed off for King Street.

✧✧ ✧ ✩

Our first stop was the barbershop, because Becky's brothers were regulars there and she knew the barber would happily allow us to post the flyer in his window. We also hit up the pharmacy, the hardware store, and a little café that sold fancy teas from around the world.

The café owner was a nice lady with long curly red hair who looked at the flyer with interest, then asked me if it was too late for her daughter, who was a sixth grader at a nearby private school, to sign up.

"It's too late for this session," I said, trying to sound professional, "but we're planning to do future performances. You should check out our website."

When we left the café, Becky said, "You have a website?" She sounded extremely impressed.

"Well, not yet," I confessed. "But we will eventually." *If there's a second show*, I added silently.

We were halfway down the block when I heard someone calling Becky's name.

"Hey! Mezan!"

Becky turned in the direction of the voice (which resulted in me losing a fair amount of umbrella coverage).

"Oh, hi, Daria!"

I instantly felt a knot form in my stomach as I looked and saw not only Daria but the whole starting lineup of the girls' soccer team headed our way.

"Sucky weather, huh?" said Daria.

"We're all going to get our nails done," Abigail Silver

reported, giggling. "Wanna come with?" She eyed me like I was a creature from another planet. "Your friend can come too, I guess."

Seriously? "Your *friend*"? Like she didn't know who I was? Abigail and I had been riding the same school bus for our entire lives. Her brother, Matthew, and I were in the same Hebrew school class!

"Thanks, but we can't," said Becky. "We're doing a really important errand."

I wondered if she'd only called it important for my benefit. Then I felt bad for wondering that.

"Oh, man, too bad," said Daria, not bothering to spare me a second glance. "Well, maybe next time. Oh, and we, like, totally missed you at the pool party last Sunday! We were really hoping you and that Austin guy would be there, but I guess he was busy too."

That Austin guy?

I was positive I'd heard her wrong.

And then . . . I was positive I hadn't. Because suddenly it made sense. Austin had known Daria's party had started at eleven thirty because he'd been invited.

That Austin guy!

That.

Austin.

Guy.

OMG!

"That Austin guy" had been invited to Daria Benson's pool party, along with Sophia Ciancio and Becky Mezan.

Okay . . . Sophia maybe wasn't a surprise, and Becky I understood. But Austin? Could it be that somewhere between dribbling soccer balls and passing notes in study hall, Daria had somehow managed to notice how blue his eyes were?

Thunder crashed above me, and for one crazy second I found myself hoping I'd be struck by lightning.

Then the soccer girls were saying their good-byes (to Becky, not me) and splashing off in a squealing, giggling group toward the nail salon.

Becky turned to me with a sheepish look. "I'm sorry."

I shrugged. What did she expect me to say?

"I'm sorry," she repeated. "Honest. The only reason I didn't tell you about the pool party was because I didn't want you to feel bad. You were so jazzed about the theater and all, I didn't want to bring you down."

I knew this was the truth. Becky understood how miserable I'd have been if I'd known she'd been invited, so she'd done the kind thing by simply not mentioning it. It wasn't a lie, technically.

"It's fine," I said, mustering up a smile. "But, just out of curiosity, since when does Daria Benson include Austin Weatherly on her high-profile guest list?"

"Since he tutored Abigail in English," Becky reported, "and kept her from failing the class. If she hadn't passed, she'd have been benched for the first half of next season, and since Abigail's their best goalie, I guess Daria decided to invite him as a thank-you. Plus, I heard Abigail saying she thinks Austin's really cute—for a seventh grader."

"Oh" was all I could think of to say.

For a long moment the only sound was the rain hissing and splattering on the umbrella above our heads. Then I heard myself say something I never thought I'd say.

"You should go to the nail salon with Daria and the others."

Becky looked confused. "Really? But what about the posters?"

"I've got only one more left. It's all right. Honest. I'm not upset." I was, a little, but what kind of a best friend would I be if I didn't let Becky go bond with her new teammates?

Besides, there was suddenly something I had to do.

"Are you sure, Anya?"

I gave my BFF my most genuine smile. "Positive."

Becky hesitated.

"Go," I said, laughing. "It'll be fun. You can get your nails

153

done in your swim team colors. Maybe they'll even paint little dolphins on your pinkies!"

"Okay," said Becky. "I'll Instagram a picture of them later."

I stood there in the downpour, watching as she and her giant umbrella took off across the street after Daria, Abigail, and the others. Then I ran half a block to the arts and crafts store. The first thing I did was ask the owner if I could hang my poster in the window.

The second thing I did was make a spur-of-the-moment decision: I unzipped my inside pocket, took out a handful of bills, and used them to buy packets of iron-on transfer paper and blank light blue T-shirts.

✫✫✫✫

At home, using Susan's poster as my template, I created what was to be the official Random Farms logo, and Dad's inkjet to print it onto the iron-on transfer sheets.

Then I locked myself in the laundry room and plugged in the iron.

The first one came out a little crooked. The second was slightly off center. But by the third, I'd gotten the hang of it, and by the time Susan had gotten home from the movies, I had finished creating custom Random Farms Kids' Theater

T-shirts.

Take *that*, Property of Chappaqua Middle School!

"Anya?" came Susan's voice from the front hall.

"Be right there."

I quickly folded up the shirts, took a clean trash bag from the box under the laundry sink, and put them inside it. I didn't want Susan to see them until I handed them out to the cast and crew, which I would do at some point during the week before the show—tech week. They were going to be an awesome surprise!

An awesome ninety-seven-dollar surprise.

I hid the bag of shirts in the closet and went to find my sister.

Because to be honest, I was dying to know if Spencer had kissed Maddie!

CHAPTER

Before I went to bed on Sunday night, I made a conscious decision not to say anything to Austin about knowing he'd been invited to Daria's. What would be the point, right? The important thing was that he'd sent his regrets and come to auditions instead. And besides, I wanted to be in the right frame of mind as we began week two of the theater.

Actually, I couldn't wait to start rehearsal on Monday morning, and I was confident that my cast would return from their weekend activities relaxed, refreshed, and ready to get back to work.

I was wrong.

The first hour was spent—or, more accurately, frittered away—on everyone recapping their weekend fun. Jane and Elle had won the three-legged race at a neighborhood barbecue, and Mia had sung the "Star-Spangled Banner" to open Sam's baseball game (so much for resting her voice!). At that same baseball game, Sam had slid into home plate to score the winning run. Problem was, he'd done it face first, scraping his cheek and giving himself a horrible black eye in the bargain.

"I hope you've got enough pancake makeup to cover that," I whispered to Maxie.

Teddy's family had gone to Jones Beach on Long Island for the weekend, and they'd brought Travis along. Both boys were sunburned almost beyond recognition, which not only made it hard for them to dance, but made them extremely grouchy as well.

We spent a full hour on the introduction number, "Comedy Tonight," which was an ensemble piece in which the cast basically marched around and shifted in and out of simple formations with the occasional arm movement. It barely qualified as a dance, it was so straightforward.

The number should have been a breeze, but after a weekend of three-legged-racing, sliding, and singing, everyone was feeling pretty sluggish. Teddy howled in pain when Jane mistakenly flung out her left arm when she should have lifted up her right one, accidentally smacking him on his badly sunburned back.

I decided we should turn our attention to costumes, and

I was delighted with Maxie's wardrobe choices! She'd done wonders with the Quandts' hand-me-downs, which she'd combined with some old costumes and castoffs she'd dug out of her own basement. The fittings were going surprisingly well.

Until Sophia got her first real look at her costume for "Castle on a Cloud."

"It's hideous," she spat.

I could see poor Maxie was a little intimidated by our resident diva. "But it's perfect for Cosette's character," she explained.

"*Hmmphf!*" Sophia turned up her nose. "Cosette's character needs to find a better place to buy her clothes!"

"Sophia," said Austin calmly. "The song is called 'Castle on a *Cloud*,' not 'Castle on Fifth Avenue.' "

"It looks like rags!"

"That's because it *is* rags," said Maxie. "Cosette is a servant. She's practically an orphan!"

"I *know* that!" Sophia snarled. "But where is it written that orphans have to dress like slobs?"

"Pretty much everywhere," I said. I took the flower-patterned dress Maxie was holding and thrust it at Sophia. It was an enormous billowy thing that used to be my mother's. The reason it was so big was that Mom had worn it when she'd been eight months' pregnant with Susan, but no way was I going to tell Sophia *that*. I was glad Maxie had had the foresight to cut the word *maternity* off the label.

"Cosette is a child," I explained, trying my best to sound directorial. "She's mistreated and hungry and afraid. But the incredible thing about her is that she never gives up dreaming. Even though she's dressed in rags, she still believes in that beautiful castle. That's what the song is about. Now, either you wear the dress or I give the solo to someone else."

Sophia glared at me for a long moment. Finally she grabbed the costume, stomped backstage, and returned a few minutes later, wearing it.

"I hate it," she snarled.

"Good," I replied. "You can use that emotion to tap into Cosette's feelings. I'm pretty sure she'd have hated living in squalor and being treated like a slave."

Sophia glowered but said nothing.

"Well done," Austin whispered, leaning in close so only I could hear. "You turned the princess into a servant . . . and you're not even a fairy godmother."

"Oh, I'm way more powerful than a fairy godmother," I whispered back with a grin. "I'm the director!"

On Tuesday a bunch of the girls stayed late to work on the sparkly backdrop for Mackenzie's solo.

On Wednesday, thanks to Susan's efficiency, the piano tuner came and saw to the old upright. This made a huge difference in the music quality. Austin was thrilled. When I asked the tuner how much I owed him, he explained that his accounting department would send a bill. I had no idea what it cost to tune a piano; at home, Mom always handled that sort of thing. I was glad we'd collected the dues money. Even though I'd made the unexpected T-shirts purchase, I was sure what was left would cover it.

The plan for Thursday was to do our first complete run-through of the show, from the opening number to the final bows (otherwise known as the curtain call). I was hoping Austin's theme song would be ready by then so we could rehearse it.

"I think we should take our bows in order of age," Sophia suggested. "Youngest to oldest."

This seemed like a reasonable arrangement. I was about to thank her for her input when I realized her suggestion was completely self-serving. As the oldest, Sophia would be the last cast member to bow . . . a spot customarily reserved for the star of the show.

"I've got a better idea," said Austin, catching on at the

same moment. "Let's go alphabetical by last name."

Sophia pursed her lips but didn't argue.

So it would be Madeline Walinsky who would take the final bow. "Is it okay if I curtsy?" she asked me. "I've always wanted to curtsy to a crowd."

"Fine with me," I said, then turned to Austin. "Maestro Weatherly, our theme song if you please!"

This sent a ripple of curiosity and excitement through the group.

"We have a theme song?"

"That's so cool!"

"I bet Austin composed it himself."

"Are there lyrics?"

"Is there a solo part?"

That last comment, not surprisingly, had come from Sophia.

Austin, who was suddenly looking very unenthusiastic, motioned for me to join him at the piano.

"What's wrong?" I asked.

"The theme song's not finished yet. I'm still working it out."

I smiled. "That's okay. For now you can just play what you've got. As long as they get the gist of it."

"I kind of wanted to keep it under wraps until it was all

done," he said. "It means a lot to me, Anya."

"It means a lot to me, too," I assured him. "How are the lyrics coming along?"

"Slowly."

I sighed. "Well, I'm not worried. You'll get them done in time."

"So . . . ," said Susan from across the stage. "Let's hear this theme song!"

Frowning, Austin sat down at the piano and placed his marked-up music sheet on the easel. He shot me a look I couldn't read, then began to play.

Of course, everyone loved it! When he finished, the whole cast cheered.

"Can you put all our names in it?" Jane asked.

"It's going to be hard to find something that rhymes with Random Farms," Gracie observed.

"It's catchy," said Elle. "But maybe it would be better if it were a ballad."

"See?" Austin grumbled to me. "*This* is why I didn't want them to hear it until it was complete."

I felt my cheeks turn pink, realizing he'd been right. I shouldn't have insisted. "I'm really sorry," I said, and I meant it. "I just really wanted to share it with them. I wanted you to put your stamp on this show!"

His only response was to take the theme song sheet music off the easel and replace it with "Comedy Tonight."

I figured that was my cue to move on. I sighed.

"Okay, people!" I called, turning back to my cast. "We're going to take it from the opening number. Places, everyone."

I dropped myself into a folding chair, prepared to watch the show from start to finish. The actors were a little hesitant at first, and very cautious, but as they moved from number to number, scene to scene, their confidence grew and their energy increased.

I was amazed at how wonderful it all looked. Sure, there were a few flubbed lines, a few missed steps, but overall, it was looking fantastic. When it was done, Austin and I leaped to our feet and applauded.

From the way he was smiling, I guessed he wasn't upset with me anymore, which was a huge relief.

"Were we really that good?" Mackenzie asked, flushing modestly.

"You were fabulous!" I said. "All of you. There's still some work to be done, but for a first run-through, it was terrific."

"Do you have any notes for us?" Teddy asked, sitting down so his legs dangled over the edge of the stage.

"Just a few." I referred to my legal pad. "Elle, you need to be a little louder. Spencer, remember to wait for the laughter to quiet down before you start your next line."

Spencer grinned. "You think I'm really gonna get some laughs?"

"Absolutely," said Austin. "Your comic timing is excellent."

"Thanks."

"Madeline," I said, wagging my finger. "Gum!"

Madeline looked so guilty, I felt compelled to quickly add that her curtsy was top-notch.

☆☆☆☆

On Friday we ran through the show twice before lunch. Then we focused on wardrobe and makeup. That morning I'd given Maxie twenty-five of our remaining thirty-three dollars and sent her to the drugstore to buy foundation, eyeliner, cotton swabs, and disposable makeup sponges. When Spencer and Eddie heard they would be expected to wear makeup, they got flustered.

"What's the big deal?" asked Sam. "It's just colored powder and some other gunky stuff. It's no different than when football players wear eye black."

"Yeah," said Travis. "It's like Halloween."

Austin assured the boys that every major Broadway

performer and movie star spent hours in the makeup chair. Finally they agreed to let Maxie make them up.

Still, when I surprised everyone by letting them go home early, Spencer and Eddie couldn't get to the restroom fast enough to wash the makeup off before setting foot outside the clubhouse. Elle was also happy to get rid of her makeup, but the rest of the girls were thrilled to be going out in public wearing mascara and eye shadow. Of course, if their moms were anything like mine, they'd be ordered into a hot shower before they could say *lip liner*!

When everyone was gone, I cleared my throat and smiled at Austin. I knew it would be a sore subject, but I was simply too curious.

"So . . . about that theme song. Any luck with the lyrics?"

He gave me a frustrated look. "A little. I managed to rhyme *laugh* with *choreograph*, but I'm not sure it's gonna stick."

"Well, don't worry," I said. "You'll get it."

"I'm planning to work on it all weekend," he promised. "Like I said, it means a lot to me."

"You'll knock it out of the park," I said confidently. "And there's a chance we'll be able to start rehearsing it on Tuesday."

"No guarantees," said Austin. "But I'll try. Those harmonies need to be worked out in my head before I can teach the cast. I don't want to do it until I can do it right."

"Okay, okay." I held up my hands like I was on the wrong end of a stickup. "No pressure."

He smiled, but only a little. "I appreciate that. And I'll see what I can do."

It was on the tip of my tongue to mention that since he had so much work to do on the theme song, it would probably be in his best interests not to accept any pool party invitations that might come along, but I was afraid he might misinterpret that comment as snarky.

Oh, who was I kidding . . . it *was* snarky. So I bit my lip and waved to him as he left.

"Have a good weekend!" he called as the door swung closed.

"Thanks!" I called back. I just didn't have it in me to say, *You too.*

☆☆☆☆

Over the weekend, Susan and I handled "the paperwork." This included making the tickets and the program on the computer.

"How many do we need?" Susan wondered aloud, her index finger hovering over the laptop's track pad.

Honestly, I had no idea. I did know there were fifty folding chairs (Austin had counted) stored under the stage in our theater. I wished there were more; the clubhouse space was certainly roomy enough for at least one hundred chairs. Not that I even dared to dream we'd have a full house.

"Let's see," I said. "There are seventeen kids, with two parents each, so that's thirty-four parents." I frowned. "But Mia and Eddie and you and I share a set of parents so that becomes . . . thirty parents total."

"I bet Nana Adele and Papa Harold will want to see the show," said Susan.

"Yes! And I'm sure all the other kids have Nanas and Papas, or grandmas and grandpas or what-have-yous who'd be interested too."

Unfortunately, this presented a far more complicated calculation. There were a lot of unknowns in the equation. Some grandparents lived far away, and others probably didn't like to drive at night.

"Well, Gracie's Yiayia and Papou live in Greece," said Susan, "so I'm thinking we can count them out."

"Austin is inviting Mrs. Warde, the English teacher, to the show."

"Ugh," said Susan. "She'll probably want to grade us on it."

"And I know the Quandts wouldn't miss it for the world."

"I think Sam said some of the kids on his baseball team might come."

"Don't forget about all those posters you put up," Susan reminded me. "I'm sure those will draw some customers."

Maybe we would have a decent-size audience after all. Or maybe we'd wind up with Nana, Papa, thirty obligated parents, and eighteen empty folding chairs. Right now it was anybody's guess.

"Make fifty programs," I said, feeling optimistic.

Susan hit the track pad, and the printer began to whir.

Truth be told, I'd be perfectly happy with fifty theatergoers. Heck, I'd be happy with five as long as somebody showed up to see what we'd accomplished.

Just so all our hard work wouldn't go to waste.

As I watched the pages zip out of the printer, I felt my fingers crossing of their own accord. *Please don't let that theater be empty on opening night*, I thought.

And it wasn't just for me I was making this wish.

It was for my cast.

CHAPTER

Tech Week had arrived. We couldn't hold rehearsal on Monday, because of the Fourth of July holiday, but I told myself this was a good thing. We all needed a break, and what could be better than a long weekend with fireworks and patriotic parades to put us all in the right mind-set? Musical theater was, after all, the great American art form.

On Tuesday I got up early and decided to make a to do list for this final and crucial week of rehearsal. It was only just beginning to sink in how close we were to opening night. The show went up on Saturday—in exactly five days. And we still had a ton of kinks to work out. The thought made me feel excited and nervous. Confident and at the same time completely and totally in over my head.

But I never turned away from a challenge. So I sat down at the kitchen table and made my checklist.

Director's TECH WEEK To Do List

1. ASK AUSTIN ABOUT THE THEME SONG!
2. Remind Madeline W. to take the gum out of her mouth before she goes onstage
3. Hand out T-shirts (surprise!)
4. Make sure restrooms are clean and stocked
5. Have Maxie H. triple-check that all straight pins have been removed from costumes after alterations
6. Write blurb about silencing cell phones and no flash photography
7. Remind Madeline W. again about the gum
8. Begin advance ticket sales
9. SERIOUSLY . . . THE THEME SONG!
10. ???

I read my list over three times but feared that once again I'd forgotten something important.

I was almost certain there was something else . . . a tenth to do item, but for the life of me, I couldn't think of what it could be. All the way to the clubhouse theater, I wracked my brain trying to think of what it could be.

One slight problem was that I had no money to use for change in the cashbox. I'd already spent ninety-seven dollars of our one hundred and thirty dollars in dues money on the T-shirts. Then I'd given Maxie twenty-five of the remaining thirty-three dollars for makeup essentials. This left me with a whopping eight bucks in our theater fund (barely enough to replace Mom's economy-size bottle of Windex). For now I would just hope that anyone who wanted to purchase tickets today came with exact change.

Lugging my trash bag full of custom Random Farms T-shirts, I unlocked the theater door and stepped inside. I knew this was the beginning of what might just be the most important week of my life. I quickly tucked the bag under the stage with the folding chairs. My plan was to hand out the shirts sometime before Friday's dress rehearsal. This way the cast could wear them during their bows while singing Austin's original theme song!

Which Austin was still working on and therefore we hadn't rehearsed yet, with or without the harmonies that may or may not be still stuck in his head.

As if by some unspoken agreement, every member of my cast (well, almost) arrived good and early—they knew this was a big day, and it did my heart good to know that they were taking it seriously. Even Sophia managed to show up on time, which for her was a major accomplishment.

After referring to my to do list, I decided that my first task was to make Madeline turn in her pack of bubble gum at the door. Then I sent Eddie to refill the soap dispensers in the restrooms.

So what hadn't I done?

I decided not to dwell on it, whatever it was. Sooner or later it would come to me.

Today was to be our first day of the process known as tech rehearsal. That was when the show was rehearsed using all the technical aspects—like sound and lighting and set changes—to be sure they would run smoothly for the performance.

For us this would be ridiculously easy, since we didn't really have all that much tech. For stage lighting there were only the simple overhead canister lights, which didn't do anything but go up and down. The only additional lighting element was the strand of holiday lights Deon had staple-gunned to the front edge of the stage. Unfortunately, there were no spotlights.

"No spotlights?" Sophia threw her hands up in disgust. "Why is this the first I'm hearing of it?"

"You would have known it," I said tightly, "if you hadn't skipped out on the first rehearsal to go to Daria's pool party."

Sophia ignored the barb. "How am I going to sing my solo without a spotlight?" she fumed. "I pictured myself haloed in a glowing circle of pale pink light."

"Sorry," said Deon, "but look at it this way: without a spotlight, people might not notice how raggedy your costume is."

Maxie shot him a look.

"Whatever!" Sophia rolled her eyes. "Just body mic me and get it over with."

"About that . . . ," said Austin.

"No mics, either?" Sophia looked stricken. "You can't be serious. First you aren't going to light me, now you won't even mic me?"

"Don't worry about it," said Teddy. "You're plenty loud enough without one."

"That's because I know how to *project*!" she screamed.

"So it's not a problem," said Austin. "You don't *need* a mic. You can project."

"That's one word for it," Susan mumbled.

"It's the principle of the thing," Sophia huffed.

Since we didn't have a stage crew, Deon and Maxie had been appointed co-stage managers; they would be responsible for changing backdrops, switching out props and set pieces, and of course, operating the curtain.

The curtain!

That was what I'd forgotten.

I felt like I'd just been punched in the gut.

"What's wrong, Anya?" asked Susan. "You look like you're gonna be sick or something."

"I never got around to finding a curtain," I confessed. "How could I forget the curtain? It's, like, the first thing people think of when they think of a theater."

No one disagreed. I vowed silently to handle it before the end of the week. I wanted a curtain. My cast wanted a curtain. Who would ever take us seriously if we didn't have a curtain?

But right now I had to focus on rehearsal.

"Let's get started," I said, clapping my hands briskly.

Everyone hurried into the wings (although without a curtain, they really weren't all that winglike). There was a cacophony of whispering, giggling, and shuffling of feet.

"It's going to have to be a lot quieter back there on opening night!" I warned.

But this accomplished nothing; in fact, it made things worse by setting off a series of overly loud *shhhhhhhhs*.

Susan and Austin lowered the old roller shades on the windows, and when Deon hit the main light switch that controlled the house lights, the whole interior of the theater turned dusky gray.

This did the trick; the noisy fidgeting from the wings stopped instantly, and a hush fell over the place.

"That's more like it," said Austin with a grin.

"Places for the opening number!" I commanded.

Everyone crept onto the shadowy stage.

"Move over, Elle."

"Teddy, you're supposed to be over there."

"No, Jane stands there. I stand here."

"How can you stand here when I'm supposed to stand here?"

"Mackenzie has to be in front. If Mackenzie's not in front, I won't remember the steps."

"Mackenzie *is* in front."

"Eddie!"

"What?"

"We haven't even started to dance, and you're already stepping on my foot."

With a sigh, I turned the main lights back on. Twelve faces turned to me.

"What's the problem?" asked Susan.

"We forgot to spike," I said.

"Spike?" Spencer repeated. "That sounds kinda dangerous."

I explained that spiking was the practice of marking

places onstage with small pieces of tape so the actors would always know exactly where to stand. Spike tape came in all different colors, and some varieties even glowed in the dark.

"So, let's spike now," Susan suggested.

"Great idea," I said. "Except we don't have any tape."

"Check the bag of art stuff my mom brought," said Deon.

I hurried over to where we'd left the shopping bags and, sure enough, there was a roll of ordinary masking tape. It wouldn't glow in the dark, but at least for the moment it would keep my performers from clobbering one another on stage.

I was just tearing off the first piece of tape when I heard a car horn out front. I looked out the box office window. A silver minivan was parked at the curb, and a black station wagon was pulling up behind it.

I checked my watch, surprised as always to see that the time had gotten away from us.

"I guess we're done for today," I said glumly. "See everyone back here tomorrow."

☆✩☆✩

Needless to say, the next day we found ourselves in a spiking frenzy. I had my actors walk through the blocking for every scene while Maxie, Deon, and I scrambled around on our hands and knees, sticking pieces of tape to the floor.

We only had to use Mrs. Becker's boring masking tape to mark the places where set pieces should be placed because Austin had surprised me with several rolls of electrical tape in a whole array of colors. Each performer got to pick out his or her own color, which would make it even easier for them to find their precise places—all they had to do was look for the X in their chosen color. Eddie picked blue *and* orange (Mets fan) for his Xs while Travis picked yellow and black to express his loyalty to the Boston Bruins.

After we'd spiked ourselves silly, we finally got around to doing the cue-to-cue.

It was, as expected, pretty simple: we basically walked the acts on and off the stage, one after the other, while Deon brought the lights up and down between every act.

Lights up. Dance. Lights down. Exit.

Lights up. Monologue. Lights down. Exit.

Lights up. Song. Lights down. Exit.

If we had had a more sophisticated system, we'd have been able to program all kinds of cool changes and effects into a computerized lighting board. I hated to admit it, but I was almost glad we didn't have one, just so Sophia wouldn't get her "pale pink glow."

Overall, I was pleased. The spike tape made things go a lot more smoothly and efficiently. Sophia complained only once through the entire exercise, which was some kind of a record, I think.

While the cast rehearsed, Susan got proactive and pushed the Quandts' donated table beneath an open window to create a box office. She made a hand-lettered sign that said **TICKETS** and propped it in the window. Five minutes later, to my surprise and delight, Becky's face appeared in the window.

"One please," she said, handing over five singles.

"Great!" cried Susan. "We're not technically open yet, but since you have exact change, we're good to go." She slid the bills into the empty cashbox and gave Becky her ticket.

"Hey!" I laughed, hurrying over to the window. "I was planning to comp you a front-row seat. That's kind of a perk of being the director's best friend."

"Thanks," said Becky, grinning. "But I'm happy to pay. From what I hear, this show is worth way more than the price of admission!"

"Come on in and look around," I said.

"Wish I could. Golf lesson. Then a tennis match. Diving practice after that!" She waved through the window and disappeared.

Susan spent the entire morning at the box office window. The good news was that a bunch of neighborhood kids came by asking about the show. The bad news was that none of them plunked five bucks down on the windowsill like Becky had. They did say they were planning to come to the show, which was very encouraging but still didn't change the fact that there were only five measly dollar bills in the cashbox.

I was working with Travis and Mackenzie on their dance number when the door opened.

"Hello there!"

I was surprised to see my mother entering the theater. I left my dancers and rushed across the theater. "Hi, Mom! What's up?"

She handed me an envelope. "This came in the mail for you," she said. "I imagine it's theater related, so I thought I'd drop it off."

I glanced at the return address in the corner of the envelope—*The Soft Peddlers, Inc., Port Chester, NY*. It took me a moment to realize it was the bill from the piano tuner. I stuffed it into my pocket, deciding I'd deal with it later when the cast was gone.

"Thanks, Mom," I said, staring purposefully at the door.

Mom laughed. "Okay, okay, I'm leaving. I know you want the show to be a big surprise."

"Hey, wait!" cried Susan. "Aren't you forgetting something?"

"What's that?"

"You forgot to buy your tickets."

"Susan!" I cried. "Mom and Dad and Nana and Papa are our guests. They get house seats for free."

"No, no," said Mom quickly, opening her purse. "Susan's right. This is a professional operation, and I'm happy to purchase our tickets. At full price."

"Good! They're five bucks apiece." Susan held out her hand with a big smile.

Four front-row seats and twenty dollars later, Mom left the theater.

And I went back to Kenzie and Travis, forgetting all about the bill in my pocket.

CHAPTER

16

When everyone was gone, Susan stood beside the old table and frowned at the cashbox, which now held twenty-five dollars. "I sure hope there's a lot more than that on opening night," she said.

"Don't worry," I said. "That's what happens with general admission. Maybe next time we should assign seats. That might create more of a buzz. You know . . . buy early, get better seats."

Susan laughed. "You never cease to amaze me with your ability to think like a theater tycoon."

The problem was, I didn't feel much like a tycoon at the moment. I'd spent nearly all our dues money on the T-shirts, and I still had to pay my parents back for the paper and the cleaning supplies. And right now it remained to be seen how much we'd earn in ticket sales.

With a jolt, I remembered the bill in my pocket and my stomach flipped over. I pulled it out and stared at it.

"Whatcha got there?" asked Austin.

"It's from the piano tuner!" I said, slipping my finger under the flap and tearing it open.

INVOICE #717213

BILL TO: MS. ANYA WALLACH

SERVICES RENDERED:

Standard Tuning..$175.00
Sticky Key Repair $45.00
(2) Broken String Replacement @ $30 ea. $60.00

Total $280.00

Two hundred and eighty dollars? I felt myself sway on my feet. There was a date on the invoice too, indicating that the Soft Peddlers would like to be paid before the end of the week.

"Anya, are you all right?" Susan sounded nervous. "You

just went completely pale."

Pale? It was a miracle I hadn't passed out! I'd never in a billion years imagined it would cost close to three hundred dollars to tune a crummy old upright piano. Then it occurred to me that maybe its being so crummy and old was precisely why it *had* cost so much to fix.

Austin raised one eyebrow. "How much?"

I showed him the invoice, being careful to let my thumb cover the "pay by" date.

He turned as pale as I had. "Wow."

"I know, right?" I shook my head. "I never expected it to be so expensive. I mean, what's this sticky key thing about?"

"It's about a key that was sticky." His expression turned guilty. "I complained to the guy about it."

"But it was *only* one key," I said. "Couldn't you have just played without it?"

Austin looked at me like I was nuts. "Um . . . no."

He was right, of course. And since the piano was our only source of music, I knew that the fee for tuning it was money well spent. It's just that it was an awful *lot* of money well spent.

"The dues will cover part of it," said Austin. "Won't they?"

"We collected one hundred and thirty bucks," said Susan. "We only need one hundred and fifty dollars more. If we sell all fifty tickets at five dollars each, that gives us . . . um"—she did the math in her head—"two hundred fifty bucks. That plus the dues money, minus . . . what? Maybe fifty bucks we owe Mom and Dad for the cleaning and office supplies we used and the twenty-five you gave Maxie? That's seventy-five. Okay . . . well, that leaves us with three hundred and five dollars. Plenty to pay the piano guys, and even a few bucks left over for"—she waggled her eyebrows at me—"I'm thinking . . . cast party!"

"I like the sound of that," said Austin.

So did I. But what they didn't know was that I'd impulsively blown ninety-seven of our one hundred and thirty dollars on extremely cool but entirely unnecessary custom cast T-shirts.

"Then again, we still have to buy a few things," Susan reminded me. "Maxie says we need bobby pins and a couple of pairs of false eyelashes. And remember in the cue-to-cue, when Madeline accidently stepped on one of the Christmas bulbs?"

"There goes the cast party." Austin chuckled.

I guess my feelings showed on my face because Austin placed a hand on my shoulder and smiled.

"Cheer up," he said. "Most businesses don't turn a profit right away. At least we haven't lost any money."

I gulped and forced a smile. "Yeah," I croaked. "At least we haven't done that."

"Look," he said, "once we have that ticket money, I'm sure we'll be able to afford the tuning cost. But dress rehearsal is in two days, and the show goes up on Saturday night. So let's just focus on the revue for now and not worry about the piano guys until after we count our earnings. Okay?"

I nodded. "Okay."

But for me, not worrying was a lot easier said than done.

That night after dinner I told my parents I was going out for a walk.

It had taken me a full hour to make my decision, and then another hour to convince myself to actually go through with it. It was almost eight o'clock when I finally left the house.

The walk to Sophia Ciancio's front door was the longest of my life.

I knocked—then immediately considered turning and sprinting back home.

But I didn't. I couldn't. I had run out of options.

A minute later the door opened.

"Anya," said Sophia, looking surprised. "What are you

doing here?"

I let out a long rush of breath. "Well, Sophia," I said glumly, "I have something I think you might be interested in."

I showed her what I'd been holding behind my back, and the corners of her mouth turned up into a cool smile. Eyes shining, she stepped aside and let me in.

✧✦✩✫

I had a very strange feeling on Thursday. All day, in fact, from the moment Susan and I had set out for the theater. I tried to tell myself it had nothing to do with the heart-wrenching business transaction I'd conducted the night before. But I hadn't had any other choice. In real theater there are *backers*, wealthy bigwigs who invest in shows. At Random Farms there was me . . . and I needed to recoup the money I had spent on those T-shirts. So I'd taken matters in my own hands and solved our financial problems the only way I could think of.

I tried to ignore the icky feeling. It was a creepy crawling sensation just below my skin. Like something bad was about to happen. I whispered this to my sister on our way to the theater, but in typical Susan fashion, she shrugged it off.

"The theatrical world is filled with superstitions," she reminded me. "You know, like that weird tradition of not being allowed to talk about fast food."

I stopped walking and looked at her like she'd lost her mind. "*What?*"

"I've heard that actors believe it's bad luck to even mention a Big Mac inside a theater." She wrinkled her nose thoughtfully. "Or maybe it's a Whopper Jr.?"

"Susan," I said, trying not to crack up. "It's *MacBeth*. And he was not a cheeseburger; he was the title character in one of William Shakespeare's great tragedies."

"Whatever," said Susan. "But seriously, isn't it silly?"

"You're probably right. I'm just being superstitious."

And by the time we'd arrived at the clubhouse theater, I was so wrapped up in thinking about what we had to accomplish in two days, I'd forgotten all about my uneasy feeling.

For most of the morning Maxie had the floor, going over her list of costume changes and reminding the actors about which zippers had a tendency to get stuck and how they should wear their hats so they would be least likely to fall off. There was also a twenty-minute seminar about the importance of wig caps and another about the health implications of sharing a makeup brush.

Then we ran through the show.

"I have an idea," said Spencer, three lines into his *Peter Pan* scene.

Maxie sighed, consulting her wardrobe notes. "If it's about switching out the green tights for basketball shorts again, you can forget it."

"No," said Spencer. "This idea is for Deon." He turned a hopeful smile to D. "How hard would it be to make me fly?"

"Fly?" said Deon, mildly surprised.

"Fly?" said Austin, in absolute shock.

"Yeah!" said Spencer. "I was reading online about the original production of *Peter Pan*. The actor—well, actress, actually—got to fly around above the stage and over the audience, and I was just thinking it would be way cool if I could do that."

"And you were thinking this one day before dress rehearsal?" I said. "Seriously?"

"D, what do you think?" Spencer prompted. "You're a whiz at this kind of thing. What would you need? Cables? Wires?"

I felt a grab in my stomach, imagining the cost of said cables and wires.

"Well, let's see," said Deon, making a show of pacing the stage and scratching his chin thoughtfully. "I guess I'd need a harness, and some really strong rope . . . and of course"—he stopped pacing and turned to glare at Spencer—"a whole lot of pixie dust!"

Chapter Sixteen

Everyone laughed except Spencer. "It was only a suggestion," he muttered.

"Take it from the top," I said.

There was a moment of panic when Austin couldn't find the sheet music for "Brotherhood of Man." I was so upset, I was on the verge of accusing Eddie of intentionally destroying it just so he could get out of doing the dance. But luckily, Susan found it before I could say anything.

Then I felt guilty for even thinking a nice kid like Eddie would ever do such a crummy thing. I confessed my fear to Austin in a whisper.

"I thought maybe he'd tried to sabotage the number," I admitted.

"Sabotage, huh? You must be awfully nervous if you're starting to accuse your actors of espionage."

"I know." I grinned. "Although, in this case, I guess you'd have to call it *thespian-age.*"

For a while things went smoothly. Better than smoothly. Perfectly, in fact. No sour notes, no missed cues. Big smiles, clear voices.

I was feeling so good about the show that I decided this was the perfect time to reveal my surprise. I opened the door under the stage and dragged out my plastic bag.

"I've got something for you guys," I said, pulling out the

first T-shirt. "It's my way of thanking you for all your hard work, and it shows that we're all in this together."

I was suddenly surrounded by a swarm of actors.

"These are awesome, Anya!" cried Gracie.

"Great color!" said Jane.

"Love the logo," said Eddie, wriggling into his.

"You should have sprung for the one-hundred-percent-cotton shirts," said Sophia, snatching one out of the bag. "But at least this shade of blue goes well with my eyes."

Susan took me by the elbow and pulled me aside to the ticket table, where a curious-looking Austin joined us.

"Anya, how did you pay for those shirts?" my sister asked.

"The usual way," I said. "With money."

"Duh. I meant what money."

I declined to answer.

Austin looked at me closely. "The dues money?"

I sighed. "Yes. Yes, I used the dues money to buy T-shirts and iron-on decal sheets, okay? But it was before I knew about the piano bill!"

"Anya . . . ," said Austin. "That puts us in a major deficit."

"It did," I said, "but I took care of it."

"How?" asked Susan. "Did you borrow money from Mom and Dad?"

"No! I didn't borrow a penny!"

The fact of the matter was that it had never even occurred to me to ask my parents for cash. I'd gotten myself into this mess, so I'd gotten myself out of it.

"We're covered," I said tersely. "So it doesn't matter how I paid."

As I walked back to my chair, I heard Sam saying, "Maybe for the next show, we can get hoodies."

Fat chance.

And then it was time to try the curtain call.

"Maxie, if it's all the same to you, I'd like the cast to wear these T-shirts for the curtain call on Saturday."

Maxie nodded. "All right with me!"

"Good," I said. "Now, let's go through the bows."

Before the words were even out of my mouth, Austin had leaped up from the piano bench. "Ready for another surprise? The theme song is ready."

I felt a surge of happiness. I'd been holding out hope that he'd complete the song in time. Austin had come through! It was hard to believe I had ever doubted him.

He was walking from actor to actor, handing out lyric sheets. "Take a minute to go over these," he said. "Read 'em through. Memorize the lyrics."

"Wow," said Teddy. "There sure are a lot of words."

Gracie eyed the page. "I was right," she said. "Nothing

does rhyme with *Random Farms*."

Under Austin's direction, the kids mumbled through the verses and chorus five or six times. After that, he herded them onto the stage, placing them, moving them around, barking out dance steps, and then changing everything and doing it all over again.

"Jeesh, Weatherly," said Deon from the wings. "Can you slow down a little? I need to figure out how I'm gonna light this."

Either Austin didn't hear Deon or he simply chose not to respond. Instead he just went right on giving directions.

"Mia, you sing the high part, okay? This line here. Can you hit a high C? Doesn't matter . . . You'll get it. Now, Travis, this part right toward the end . . . I want you to sing it in that cool British accent you were messing around with yesterday."

Susan looked at me. "British accent?" she whispered. "He's kidding, right?"

I certainly hoped so. But suddenly I wasn't sure.

In the next second, Austin had launched into his plans for the harmonies. I wasn't a trained vocalist, so of course I was lost, but I could tell from the look on Sam's face that even to him they sounded impossible.

"Everybody got it?" Austin asked with a big smile.

Nobody did.

But that didn't stop him from hopping down from the stage and running back to the piano. "Okay, people. Here we go. Ready, Mia? Sophia? Jane, just try to keep up, and, Mackenzie, if you can maybe bang out a pirouette or two during the bridge that would awesome."

His fingers hit the keys like his fingers were on fire, and music filled the room.

Once again I was struck by how amazing the melody was. Austin sang loudly, leading them, belting out the brilliant lyrics, which of course he knew by heart.

The song was great. Austin was great.

But the activity onstage was a whole other story.

Kids were tripping over one another trying to remember the complicated moves and intricate steps, not to mention the lyrics, which they had seen for the first time only five minutes earlier. Nobody remembered the tune. Nobody understood the harmonies.

They were trying. Really trying.

But it was an unqualified disaster.

When Austin finished playing the song, he turned to me with a glowing smile. "Shall we try it one more time?"

One *more*? I thought. *How about one* million *more?* Because, clearly, that was what it would take for our cast to learn this incredibly intricate song and dance. The problem was, we didn't have time for a million more tries. This was an ambitious song—a terrific, dynamic song. And slapping it together at the last minute would never do it justice.

This was our theme song. And it deserved better than that.

An ache began deep in my heart because I didn't want to say what I was about to say.

For a moment I just sat there on my folding chair. Then, slowly . . . very slowly . . . I shook my head.

"No, Austin," I said.

"No?" Austin looked baffled. "You don't want to try it again? But it needs a little more work."

"It needs a *lot* more work," I corrected. "And a lot more time." I lifted one shoulder in a sad shrug. "I'm sorry, Austin. We just can't put your song in the show. "

Onstage, the entire cast went perfectly still. Someone gasped. Fourteen pairs of wide eyes gaped at me, then at Austin.

Austin's face was blank, as though he couldn't believe what he'd just heard. "What did you just say?"

"I said we can't use the theme song. Not this time. It's too much to learn on such short notice."

Austin's jaw flexed, and his eyes turned cold. "But you were the one who kept bugging me to finish it," said Austin, glowering. "You were the one who rushed me to get it done!" He made a face and mimicked me in a high voice, "*Oh, you can do it, Austin. Just hurry up and finish it, Austin. We need it for the curtain call, Austin.*"

"I didn't do that!"

"Yes, you did!" he snapped. "You said you wanted a theme song."

"I did want it!" I snapped back, then shook my head and corrected myself. "I *do* want it. Because it's fantastic, and I know how hard you worked, and honestly, I'm grateful. But I was wrong to push you. I should have known there wouldn't be enough time to learn it."

Austin whirled to face the cast, who was standing like a dozen deer caught in a highway's worth of headlights. "Do *you* think it's too hard?" he asked them in a tight voice. "Do you guys think it's too much *trouble* to learn the theme song I spent the last three weeks working on because Anya told me to?"

Teddy looked down at his sneakers. Elle shrugged. Jane, Madeline, and Mia pretended to study their fingernails. Finally Travis piped up.

"The harmonies are a little complicated."

"And the dance steps are kind of confusing," said Spencer.

I crossed the floor so that I was face-to-face with Austin.

195

"I'm sorry. But I'm the director. And the director directs. So I'm making a decision for the good of the show. No theme song."

"Wow," said Austin, dragging his hand through his hair. "Just . . . wow! This is unbelievable. You know how hard I worked on that song. It was the one thing in this whole stupid show that was mine."

"That's not true," I said quickly. "You wrote the whole revue."

"I cobbled the whole revue. Big deal."

"It *is* a big deal."

"You know what I think?" Austin leaned toward me, and I could see his eyes were filled with anger. Or maybe it was pain. "I think you're just taking my song out of the show because you don't want to share the spotlight with anybody. You keep talking about 'my show, my show.' Well, you didn't do it all by yourself, ya know, Miss Big Shot Director!"

Somebody snorted at that. My money was on Sophia.

"I know it's not just *my* show," I said defensively. "It's *our* show." I planted my hands on my hips. "But it just happened to be *my* idea!"

Austin narrowed his eyes. "You're so full of yourself, Anya!"

"Me!" I had all I could do to keep from stamping my foot.

196

"*I'm* full of *my*self? I'm not the one who gets invited to A-list pool parties and then thinks he's too cool to tell his friends about it!"

This brought him up short. "You know about that?"

"Yes, I know about that. I know you got invited to Daria's and then lied to me about it!"

"I didn't lie!"

"Well . . . you didn't tell the truth!"

Austin threw his hands up in the air and shot me a scathing look. "Look who's calling who a liar! At least *I* didn't go out and spend all our dues money behind everybody's back!"

I felt as though I'd been slapped. "It wasn't like that! I was just trying to do something nice."

"And you wound up doing something stupid!"

"Okay, f-fine," I sputtered, the fury rising in my chest, threatening to turn to tears. "So I splurged! So I bought some T-shirts. So sue me! Sue me!"

He gave me a mocking smile. "Thank you, Nathan Detroit."

I could have screamed! *Guys and Dolls* humor? Now? Was he serious? I couldn't believe this was the same boy who'd sat on my front porch making plans for our theater. I took a long breath.

"The song goes," I said.

"Then so do I!" With that, Austin stomped to the piano, grabbed his sheet music, and bolted out the door.

Once again silence fell over the theater. No one said a word. No one even breathed. I suddenly realized that theater superstitions weren't silly at all. The creepy feeling I'd had that morning had been right.

Something bad *had* happened.

Something very, very bad.

Don't cry, I told myself. *Don't cry. It's not professional to cry.*

Without turning to face the twelve astonished actors who stood staring at me from the stage, I waved my hand in a gesture of dismissal.

"We're done for the day," I said in a level voice. "You can all go home."

Then, with my head high, my shoulders back, and my knees shaking, I walked out the door.

I went straight to bed. Mom called me for dinner, but I wasn't hungry. Sometime around nine o' clock Susan knocked.

"You okay?" she asked through the door.

I didn't answer.

All I could think about was that horrible scream fest between Austin and me. We were supposed to be working together, but instead we'd turned on each other and said horrible things that had nothing to do with the Random Farms Kids' Theater at all. We must have looked ridiculous! We'd acted like idiots.

He was right. . . . I'd been too pushy. I'd forgotten about the creative process; I'd completely disrespected his artistic integrity. But then he'd been too sensitive and closed-minded. He refused to see that there just wasn't enough time to learn the song, to perform it the way it should be performed. He was disappointed. Maybe even hurt.

But I was hurt too. I wasn't full of myself. I was the director.

Why couldn't he just listen to me?

And worst of all . . . worse than his bringing up the T-shirts and my bringing up the pool party . . . was that somehow we'd both forgotten about what was really important.

The show.

It was two a.m. before I finally felt my eyes grow heavy. At last I fell asleep . . . wondering what might happen tomorrow.

Would Austin even show up? Would anyone?

And could I blame them if they didn't?

☆☆☆☆

When I arrived at the clubhouse on Friday morning, Austin was already there, seated at the piano.

Frankly, I was surprised to see him.

I was even more surprised to see Becky sitting on the bench beside him.

"Uh, hi."

They turned in unison. Becky smiled at me. She, of course, looked stunning. With the exception of that rainy Saturday when we'd traipsed up and down King Street, her whole summer vacation had been spent either at the golf course or the town pool, so her skin was this golden bronze color. The closest thing I'd seen to sunshine in the last three weeks were our phony footlights.

Austin and I were careful not to make eye contact.

"This place looks awesome, Anya," Becky said, hopping up from the piano bench to give me a hug. "I'm on my way to a swim meet in Katonah. The diving coach has me doing my first double back flip today, and my relay team has a super-good chance of breaking the league record in our age group."

"That's awesome."

"I just stopped in to offer to help out tomorrow night. Do you need ushers? Maybe I can help sell tickets at the door."

I was still distracted by the fact that Austin and I had yet to acknowledge each other. Clearly, he was still furious with me.

And that was making me furious with him. Furious with a side of really, really awkward. I tried to stay focused on Becky.

"That would be great," I said, hoping to sound enthusiastic and grateful. "You can help in the box office and show people to their seats."

"I'll wear a red vest or something so I'll look like a real Broadway usher."

"You'll look great no matter what you wear," Austin

blurted out. Then he blushed and hastily turned his attention back to the piano keys.

Becky, who in addition to being athletic and beautiful was also pretty instinctive about social situations, seemed to understand that there was something uncomfortable happening between Austin and me. Her eyes went from where his head was bent low over the piano keys, to my hands, which I was wringing.

"Okay, then," said Becky. "So . . . uh . . . I've got to get going, but I'll see you tomorrow night."

"Good luck with your relay, Beck."

"Thank you. And good luck to you, too!"

At the sound of this phrase, I forgot all about the weirdness with Austin. My blood went ice-cold. "No!" I shouted. "Don't say that. Don't *ever* say that! Take it back! Please. Take it back now."

"Anya!" Becky was looking at me as if I'd completely lost my mind. "What's the matter with you? Why wouldn't you want me to wish you good—"

"Stop!" Without thinking, I reached out to press my hand over her mouth, desperate to trap those horrible, terrible words inside.

Austin sprung up from the piano bench and hurried over to where I was practically suffocating my best friend. "It's an old theater superstition," he explained, gently removing my palm from Becky's face. "You never say goo— Uh, what you said. You say 'break a leg' instead."

Becky looked mortified. "Oh my gosh, I'm so sorry! I didn't know. I didn't mean to jinx you. Honest."

"Of course you didn't mean to jinx us," said Austin sweetly. "I mean, how would you know about theater quirks? You play soccer and swim and dive and stuff. And I'm betting the last thing you'd ever want to say to a gymnast or a soccer player is 'break a leg,' right?"

"That's very true." Becky gave him her most beautiful smile. "A fractured fibula would make it awfully hard to score a goal."

"Yes, it would," said Austin, grinning like a dope.

Meanwhile, I had no idea what a fibula even was, let alone that it could be fractured.

Now Becky turned her dazzling smile toward me. "Break a leg, Anya," she said earnestly. "Break two!"

By this point, I'd managed to collect myself enough to return Becky's smile. "Thanks," I said. "And sorry I flipped out. It's just . . . well, today's a big day. Dress rehearsal. And the play is tomorrow. So I guess I'm just a little jumpy."

"I totally get it," said Becky. "And speaking of jumpy, there's a three-meter board in Katonah with my name on it, so I'd better hustle." She gave Austin a dainty wave and a big grin. "Bye, Austin."

"See ya, Becky." The boy actually looked like he was going to melt.

When Becky was gone, I swept my eyes over the fifty empty chairs in their neat, orderly rows and felt a prickle of fear creeping up my spine. I could still hear Becky's words echoing in the warm air.

Good luck . . . Good luck . . . Good luck.

To me, they sounded like a curse.

As the actors arrived, Austin and I retreated to separate sides of the theater. I forced myself to greet everyone with a cheerful "good morning," and I tried to ignore the feeling of dread that had begun to gnaw at my guts.

But even as I smiled at my happy, eager cast, I couldn't shake the feeling that we were all doomed.

✧✧✦✩

Here was how dress rehearsal went:

Jane had a slight but immediate allergic reaction to her stage makeup, and while Maxie was frantically trying to wash it off, Travis decided to do his own hair and accidentally sprayed hairspray in Spencer's eyes.

"I'm blind!" Spencer shrieked. "Help! I'm blind!"

"You're not blind," I assured him, leading him to the boys' restroom to rinse out his eyes. "Worst that'll happen is your eyelashes will be stiff for the rest of the day."

Which reminded me: I still hadn't purchased the false eyelashes Maxie had requested. Or the bobby pins or the bottled water or . . .

"Anya?"

I turned to see Deon standing behind me, wringing his hands.

"Let me guess. You blew a fuse."

"Yeah. How'd you know?"

"I'm the director," I said with a sigh. "That's what I do."

Mr. Healy had to be called in to check the electrical circuits. This took up several minutes of precious rehearsal time, but at least he was able to fix the problem.

Mackenzie had to run home because she'd brought the dance bag that held her pointe shoes instead of the one where she kept her jazz shoes. This took fifteen whole minutes, and when she got back, her hair was all sweaty and had to be redone.

I wish I could say things improved when we started the actual rehearsal, but . . . nope. They didn't. In fact, they got worse.

During the opening number, most of the masking tape we'd used to mark the stage wound up sticking to the bottoms of the girls' character shoes.

Gracie flubbed the words of her monologue three times, and that was before she'd even gotten to the second line.

Sam forgot the steps during his dance routine, so he improvised with some very cutting-edge break-dance moves. Unfortunately, Sam wasn't an especially accomplished break-dancer, which was why he wobbled out of his head spin, landed on his face, and knocked a tooth loose. On the upside, it was a baby tooth. On the downside, he bled all over his costume, and I had to send Susan home to get Mom's laundry pretreater stain stick so Maxie could remove the blood from Sam's costume shirt.

When it was Mia's turn to sing her solo, I was delivered some extremely bad news.

"I lost my voice," she croaked.

"You *what*?"

"I think I've got laryngitis," she explained in a hoarse whisper. "Or maybe it's just nerves."

I quickly called home and told Susan that in addition to the stain remover, we were going to need hot tea and lots of it. "Herbal," I instructed. "With honey."

Teddy's fake moustache fell off. Twice.

Elle spilled lemonade all over the sheet music to "Maybe."

Madeline got bubble gum stuck in her wig.

Finally it was Sophia's turn to take the stage for "Castle on a Cloud." Austin played the intro, and I watched as Sophia's silhouette floated onto the darkened stage.

On cue, Deon brought the lights up.

When I saw Sophia, I blinked. Then I squinted. Then I screamed. "Sophia Ciancio, what on earth are you wearing?"

She gave me a snooty smile. "My father bought it for me yesterday at Bloomingdale's just for the show. You like it?"

Of course I liked it. I *loved* it. It was gorgeous. Dazzling even, this shimmery cream-colored party dress with a flouncy hemline and pink sequins all over it. It was stylish and elegant and, I was sure, incredibly expensive. But what it *wasn't* . . . was the Cosette costume Maxie had made.

"Go back to the dressing room and change," I ordered in a tight voice. "Right now."

Sophia folded her arms and looked down her nose at me. "No."

"Sophia . . ."

"I hate that stupid raggedy dress. I'm not wearing it."

I was furious! I had just opened my mouth to inform Sophia that I would be more than happy to give her solo to somebody else when I remembered that the only somebody else who could sing "Castle on a Cloud" as well as Sophia could was currently seated on folding chair number forty-nine, sipping herbal tea with honey and sounding like a frog with tonsillitis.

Judging by the triumphant smirk on Sophia's face, she knew it too.

By now everyone in the theater had gone utterly silent and had stopped whatever they were doing to watch the dramatic standoff between Sophia and me.

I stared at her for a long moment. Then, without taking my eyes off Sophia, I said, "Jane?"

Jane poked her head out from backstage. "Yes, Anya?"

"You've got your solo. You're singing 'Castle on a Cloud.' "

I heard a gasp and guessed it was Susan. But I stood my ground and turned to meet Jane's wide-eyed expression. "You know the words?"

"Yes, but . . ."

"Do you have a problem with wearing rags?"

"Not at all, but . . ."

"Then you can take Sophia's place tomorrow night and sing Cosette's song."

"B-but . . . what about that whole 'scale-of-one-to-ten' th-thing?" Jane sputtered. "You said I don't have the right amount of solo potential."

"To be perfectly honest," I said gently, "you don't. But I would much rather have someone with your dedication and enthusiasm perform the song, even if it's not perfect, than someone who cares more about herself than the show and thinks she can bully the director."

Jane looked happy and terrified at once.

Sophia looked like she might go up in flames.

"You can get off the stage now, Sophia," I said, hoping my voice would not betray the fact that I was literally shaking in my shoes.

"Fine!" Sophia said through her teeth. Then she looked beyond me toward the doorway. "Make sure you put that in your article, Mr. Jefferies," she said.

Confused, I turned to see who she'd addressed that last statement to and saw a gray-haired man standing by the ticket table. "Mr. Jefferies" was holding a notepad and a camera, and he had a press pass attached to a lanyard that hung around his neck.

I whirled back to face Sophia. "You invited a reporter?" I said with a gasp.

"No, you did," she said smugly. "Remember when my father gave you permission to use this place and you told Ms. Bradley your theater would make a good story for the *Chronicle*? Well, she took you seriously and sent Mr. Jefferies, who, by the way, is not just any reporter. He's also the drama critic. Ms. Bradley even promised to put our picture on the front page. And if you think I would ever appear in the newspaper wearing a dress made of rags, you're crazy."

"Well, now you're not going to appear in the newspaper at all," said Austin in a brittle voice.

"Maybe not," said Sophia. "But Anya is. And I bet Mr. Jefferies is going to write all about what a disaster this dress rehearsal has been. Then everyone in town is going to know that, as a director, Anya Wallach is a complete and total failure!" She let out a nasty little cackle. "I mean, c'mon! You call this a theater? It doesn't even have a curtain!"

I spun around to look at the reporter, who was furiously jotting notes on his pad.

And then . . .

I ran.

CHAPTER

I made it as far as our front porch before the tears came. I threw myself onto one of the wicker chairs and cried.

I cried because I'd worked harder on the Random Farms Kids' Theater than I'd ever worked on anything in my entire life, and I still hadn't been able to make it work.

I cried because Eddie and Madeline and Travis and all the other kids had trusted me. They'd put their whole hearts and souls into this show, and I'd let each and every one of them down.

I cried because Austin had wasted the first three weeks of his summer vacation on a theatrical revue when he should have been writing his brilliant original musical, and because Susan had stepped up and proved herself to be not only an amazing assistant but the best little sister a girl could ask for, and I had only proven myself to be exactly what Sophia

Ciancio had said I was.

A failure.

It was just too much. It was soccer tryouts all over again, only this time it was much, much worse. Because this time, I cared.

"Anya?"

I didn't look up right away because I knew my eyes were red and swollen, and there was a very good chance my nose was running.

"Anya," Austin repeated. "Look at me."

There was no avoiding it. I knew Austin would stand there forever if he had to, which, if I were being honest, was actually one of the things I liked best about him. So I used the back of my sleeve to wipe my face, took a good hard sniffle, and finally lifted my head.

"You were right."

I gave him a cautious look. "About Sophia?"

"Well, yeah. That too. But I meant"—he took a deep breath, then turned up his palms—"you were right about the theme song."

I blinked at him, wondering if maybe I'd misheard. "I was?"

He grinned. "You know you were. And the thing is, I knew it too. I just couldn't bring myself to give up without a fight."

I straightened up, pulling the chair's throw pillow into my lap and fiddling with the fringe trim. "I wasn't asking you to give up," I said softly. "I was just asking you to be patient. The song was too good to be wasted like that. Actually"—I gave him a tentative smile—"by saying no, I think I was paying you a compliment."

"Thank you. And I'm sorry."

"You're welcome. And I'm sorry too. You're an artist, and I should have never tried to rush you. And I should have never brought up Daria's party." I felt my cheeks flush bright red. "That was really immature of me."

"Maybe," he said. "But I kind of get it."

I sighed.

"You okay?" he asked.

"Not really," I said with a loud sniff. "Today was a mess. I'm sorry I freaked out back there, but everything was going so horribly wrong. Bloody teeth, blown fuses . . . reporters!"

"Yeah," Austin chuckled. "But you've got to admit, it was pretty cool to actually have the paparazzi there."

"I can't believe there's going to be an article in the *Chronicle* about what a pathetic idiot I am!"

"Hmmm," said Austin, pulling a piece of notepaper out of his pocket and studying it. "Doesn't say anything about anybody being a pathetic idiot here."

I frowned at the paper. "What's that?"

"Mr. Jefferies's notes. After you left, I asked him if he was really going to write his article about the hairspray and the bubble gum and the party dress. And d'ya know what he said?"

I was almost afraid to ask. "What?"

"He said he'd never seen a twelve-year-old handle a situation with as much poise and maturity as you handled Sophia's refusal to change costumes. He said you were a true professional and a visionary, too. He couldn't believe what we'd done with that dusty barn and the hand-me-down wardrobe, and he said what you've created in three short weeks most adults couldn't accomplish in three whole months. He was so impressed, he said he already had the whole article written in his head, which was why he was able to give me some of his notes."

"Can I see those, please?"

Austin handed me the small sheet of paper, which I used to blow my nose.

This totally cracked Austin up. And the sound of his laughing made me feel much better.

"Mr. Jefferies reminded me of something," Austin continued. "Another old theatrical superstition I'd forgotten about."

"The one about saying 'the Scottish play' instead of '*MacBeth*'?" I guessed.

"No, Shakespeare, not that one. The one that says that the bigger disaster the dress rehearsal is, the bigger success the play will be."

I felt my heart leap in my chest. "That's right! When I was in *Annie*, the director even made up a little poem about it: 'Bad dress? Don't stress! When rehearsal flops, the show is tops!' "

"Clever," said Austin. "I wish I'd written that."

"I think after what happened today, we can safely assume that *Random Acts of Broadway* might turn out to be one of the greatest shows ever."

"If not *the* greatest," Austin agreed.

I jumped up from the wicker chair, all business. "Let's go back. We still have to run the closing number and I want to see how Mia's throat feels and—"

"Wait." Austin suddenly had a weird look on his face.

"What's wrong?"

"Um, well, I think maybe we shouldn't go back just yet."

"Why not?"

"Because . . . because it might be better for you to get some fresh air first. We can take a walk to the drugstore. You still have to get those false eyelashes, right? And while we're in town, we can hang up a few more posters."

"Are you sure? Austin, the show opens tomorrow. There's so much to do."

"I know, but I think you could use a little break. Clear your head. Susan can handle things for an hour or so. Maybe we can even stop by the coffeehouse for a while. My treat this time."

I laughed. "Well, how can I refuse that?"

"You can't. Let's go."

He pointed to the door, and we were on our way.

☆✲✫☆

An hour later Austin and I were walking up the brick path to the theater. I was holding a bag from the drugstore containing two pairs of extra-long false eyelashes, a package of bobby pins, a Snickers bar for Susan (to thank her for running things in my brief absence), and a pack of bubble gum for Madeline to replace the one I'd confiscated . . . which I would not present to her until *after* the show.

I was feeling great as we approached the door. The icy cold Coke had refreshed and energized me, and I was ready to get back to work.

I took a deep breath and stepped into the theater. Then I

stopped in my tracks because the place was completely silent. And empty.

I felt a surge of panic.

"Where's my cast? Did they quit? Where is everybody?"

Austin grinned. "Why don't you check up there . . . behind the curtain?"

As he said this, I heard the sound of pulleys creaking as a billowing curtain unfurled from above, falling gracefully to conceal the stage. Just like a real Broadway theater.

I couldn't believe what I was seeing. "Austin, when . . . how . . . ?"

But I was unable to finish my question because a huge lump had formed in my throat. I could only stare. The curtain had been fashioned from the old sheets the Quandts had been planning to donate to charity. But there was much more to it than that. Brightly colored letters, neatly cut from Mrs. Becker's felt scraps, had been stitched into the fabric, forming a perfect arc that spelled out the words **THE RANDOM FARMS KIDS' THEATER**.

"Now, Deon!" Austin called.

More pulley noise. I watched as the one-of-a-kind curtain crinkled itself upward like a fancy window shade to reveal my entire cast assembled onstage behind it, smiling their heads off.

"Surprise!" they hollered.

I opened my mouth, then closed it. I tried again. On my third attempt I finally got some words out. "You guys!" I cried. "Oh, wow!"

"Do you like it?" asked Mackenzie.

"We hung it up while you were gone," said Eddie.

"We cut out the letters and sewed them on ourselves," said Susan, grinning broadly.

"It's incredible!" I breathed. "But the curtain . . . who made the curtain?"

It was then I noticed the portable sewing machine on the ticket table. A second later Mrs. Quandt popped out from backstage, her eyes shining. "Do you like it?" she asked.

"Oh yes!" I cried. "Yes, yes, yes! And thank you! Thank you, everyone."

"No, Anya," said Jane, stepping forward to give me a hug. "Thank *you*!"

CHAPTER

Here was what happened on the afternoon of opening night:

Sam's loose tooth fell out.

Mia got her voice back completely, so it probably *had* just been nerves and not something more serious. Still, since Susan was the one who'd brewed the tea and added the honey, she chose to take full credit for Mia's miraculous recovery. Mia and I chose to let her.

During our lunch break, Mr. Healy showed up with a certified electrician and informed me that it was high time a brand-new electrical panel was installed in the barn, and this would basically guarantee there wouldn't be any more blown circuits.

I felt a wave of panic. A new electrical panel was probably a very expensive upgrade, and thanks to bobby pins and sticky piano keys, the Random Farms Kids' Theater was pretty close to broke. I explained this to Mr. Healy.

He gave me a snort and a gruff look. "Nobody's askin' you to pay for it, girly. I'm in charge of the neighborhood common spaces, and I decide when things need improvement. The whole cost'll be comin' straight out of the association's petty cash fund."

I was so pleased, I actually offered Mr. Healy a high five. To my shock, he high-fived me back. "Thanks," I said.

"Yeah, yeah," he grumbled. Then, as Mr. Healy escorted the electrician to the barn's cellar, he turned over his shoulder, gave me a wink, and said, "Break a leg, kid."

I had no idea how he knew to say that instead of good luck, but I was awfully glad he did!

Ten minutes after the house had officially opened, I was in the girls' restroom, smearing on some lip gloss Maxie had given me. I'd left Susan and Becky to handle ticket sales and had ducked into the restroom for a few minutes to get myself (as Papa Harold might say) "dolled up."

Three minutes later Jane came in holding what had formerly been Sophia's raggedy Cosette dress.

"Anya, if it's all right with you, I'd rather not sing 'Castle on a Cloud' tonight."

I stopped mid-gloss smear and stared at her. Was she kidding? Was this a joke? I couldn't tell. I was about to ask, but she hurried on.

"I was thinking about what you said the day the cast list went up. So I've been listening to Mia's and Sam's and Sophia's incredible voices these last few days, and I realized something."

"What's that?"

"I realized . . . that I'm not ready yet."

I was so glad she'd said "not ready" instead of "not good enough." After yesterday I knew better than anyone how it felt to be afraid of not being good enough, and I would never want anyone in my cast to ever feel that way. Jane may not have been a natural-born singer, but I knew that with some patience and maybe a little coaching, she could eventually improve a whole lot.

"Okay, Jane," I said. "If that's what you want."

Jane smiled. In fact she looked a little relieved. "It is. Definitely. Now, about Sophia . . ."

Uh-oh. "What about her?"

"She really wants to sing the solo, and she's agreed to wear the raggedy dress. . . . That is, if it's all right with you."

I looked over Jane's head and saw Sophia peeking in through the restroom door.

"She's sorry," said Jane.

"I'm going to need to hear that from her," I said, putting

the cap on the lip gloss and slipping it into my pocket.

There was a heavy sigh from the other side of the door. A moment later Sophia entered the bathroom. She was holding something behind her back.

"I'm sorry for our . . . misunderstanding yesterday," she said. "I'd really like to sing the song."

For a split second I considered saying no. I was the director, after all. But I knew that wasn't what real theater was about. And besides, as I'd told Austin, I was never good at being bossy.

"You've got your solo," I said with a nod.

Sophia nodded back, then handed me what she'd been hiding behind her.

"I thought you might want this," she said, "in case you're thinking of starting a Random Farms scrapbook. It's an advance copy of tomorrow's *Chappaqua Chronicle*. Ms. Bradley gave it to me."

The headline nearly knocked me over.

LOCAL GIRL FORMS YOUTH THEATER.
GREAT THINGS EXPECTED.

Beneath this boldly printed vote of confidence was a photo . . . of me, Austin, and Susan! It was a candid shot, taken near the piano. We were looking over sheet music and smiling. The photographer must have snapped it just before we'd started our disastrous dress rehearsal.

"Thanks for this," I said. Then, before I could do anything I'd regret—like hugging Sophia Ciancio—I walked out of the girls' room. . . .

And—to my great surprise and indescribable joy—straight into a fully packed house!

It was one of the most awesome sights I'd ever seen. Every last one of those fifty folding chairs was occupied and, to my shock, behind the last row of chairs were at least fifty more people standing. They were parents, as expected, but also siblings and teachers and teammates and friends. I saw Mrs. Warde with her husband, and the Quandts with their grown-up daughters and their husbands. There were more grandparents than I could possibly count. The lady from the teas-of-the-world café was there with her private-school daughter. Even Daria Benson and Abigail Silver and the entire starting lineup of the girls' soccer team were there. Gracie's cute older brother had brought his cute girlfriend.

The electrician who'd replaced our circuit panel was there

with his wife and kids, as was the barista who'd rung up my and Austin's sodas yesterday at the coffeehouse. Sam's baseball buddies took up an entire row of folding chairs, and Becky's whole family was there, as was the *Chappaqua Chronicle*'s editor in chief, Ms. Bradley, who was seated beside the illustrious drama critic and all-around good guy, Mr. Jefferies.

And of course, my mom and dad and Papa Harold and Nana Adele were sitting right up front, looking as proud as could be in the very best seats in the house.

The most incredible part was that no one looked as if they'd been dragged here kicking and screaming. They all looked as if they truly wanted to come to this world-premiere performance of the musical revue called *Random Acts of Broadway*! All of them! Even Daria Benson.

"Isn't it amazing?" cried Becky, rushing over to me. "Susan and I have been selling tickets like crazy. When we ran out of chairs, she decided to charge two dollars for standing-room only. But don't worry; Mr. Healy says it's not a violation of the fire codes or anything. So you won't get arrested."

I laughed. "Glad to hear it."

"I knew you could do it," she said.

I didn't see any point in telling her that, less than twenty-four hours ago, I had thought exactly the opposite.

Austin was taking his seat on the piano bench. Susan

joined him; her job would be turning the pages for him during the performance. We all exchanged smiles, then I told Becky I'd see her after the show, and hurried backstage where my whole cast, including Sophia, was waiting for me.

They looked nervous.

And excited.

And nervous.

But most of all, they looked *ready*.

In theater, it's sort of a tradition for the director to say something inspiring on opening night. So on my walk over I'd prepared a long fancy speech in my head. It was all about the importance of teamwork and the magic of theater and the satisfaction of a job well done. It included advice and reminders and all sorts of other directorial wisdom I thought I should share before I sent them out onto that stage.

But now that it was time to express it all, I decided on something else entirely. Something that, in its own way, encompassed all that other stuff . . . and more.

"You guys are the best," I said. "I may have been the one who dreamed up this theater, but not one single bit of it could have happened without all of you. We've worked really hard, but somewhere along the way, it stopped feeling like work and started feeling more like . . . well, maybe this sounds cheesy, but . . . it started to feel like it was all meant to be."

"Doesn't sound cheesy to me," said Teddy, grinning.

"Me either," said Maddie, spitting her gum into a tissue.

"This all started because I wanted to be on a team," I continued. "And I wound up being on the best team I could have ever asked for. So, thanks."

"Showtime," said Eddie.

"Let's do this!" I cried.

Deon was ready at the light controls. I gave him a nod, and the house lights went down. The murmuring and whispering of the audience faded to silence.

"Places," I said.

My cast took the stage. In a moment I would slip out from the wings, tiptoeing through the shadowy house to take my place in the back, where I would enjoy the show.

Our show.

Heart racing in my chest, I turned to Maxie (whose hands were already clasped expectantly around the pulley rope) and whispered the words I had been waiting to say my whole life.

"Curtain up!"

Maxie gave a mighty pull on the rope, and the curtain sailed upward. Deon hit a switch and the stage was suddenly alive with light. Piano music filled the theater, and twelve incredibly dedicated, talented kids—my actors . . . my *friends*—began to perform, dancing and singing with all their hearts.

In the audience I saw people smiling and tapping their feet.

For them, this was the start of an unforgettable show.

For me, it was the start . . . of *everything*.

CHAPTER

20

I had never heard such a complete quiet.

The clubhouse theater was empty now, except for me, seated dead center in the front row, looking at the dark stage. Everyone had gone to the ice cream place with their families to celebrate our success over milk shakes and sundaes.

I suppose the reason this quiet seemed so quiet was because a mere thirty minutes ago, people had leaped to their feet to cheer and applaud and shout, "Bravo!" A few of those people had even had tears in their eyes. My mom, for one. And Mrs. Warde. And me. The show had been *that* good.

Although that wasn't to say there weren't a few bloopers. If someone had asked me yesterday how I would have reacted to mistakes in the performance, I probably would have said I'd be horrified. But when they actually happened, I was surprised to find that I was able to let them go. It was like I could finally see the bigger picture. It didn't have to be perfect; it just had to be amazing. And besides, the little mistakes had felt almost like inside jokes, because no one in the audience could have possibly noticed them. The crowd hadn't known that in the *Oliver!* scene, Sam had been wearing Eddie's Dodger costume while Eddie had been dressed in Sam's Oliver clothes, or that Gracie had left out three whole lines of her Veruca Salt monologue from *Willy Wonka*. Teddy's mustache had been on upside down, so it'd looked less like an old-time handlebar and more like some wacky overgrown goatee; Mia had forgotten one whole verse of "Maybe"; and in the *Fantasticks* dance, Travis and Mackenzie had bumped heads not once but twice.

But besides the actors themselves, only Austin and Susan and I had been aware of these minor glitches, and somehow we just knew that in the scheme of things, they didn't really matter.

After the final bow—and Madeline's perfect curtsy—the audience had milled around on the clubhouse lawn to wait for the cast to come outside. Austin and I had wound our way through the throng, listening gleefully as parents and grandparents and neighbors and friends had talked about our show. The ones who'd recognized us (like the Quandts, and Mr. and Mrs. Kim for example) had stopped us to gush about how impressed they'd been and to congratulate us on a job well done. But for me, it had been almost more exciting to overhear the theatergoers who didn't know who Austin and I were (like aunts and uncles from out of town). They'd been blown away by what we'd achieved. Most of them had been flat out shocked that we'd been able to put on such an entertaining show.

"Should we be insulted?" Austin had whispered to me.

"Nah. It's a compliment. I mean, let's face it, a bunch of middle schoolers putting on a top-notch revue all by themselves is definitely not something that happens every day."

"True," said Austin.

Then the cast had burst out of the clubhouse, and the cheering had started all over again. My actors had accepted hugs and bouquets, and I couldn't have been prouder.

But for one second, one teeny, tiny sliver of a moment, I couldn't help feeling the slightest twinge of envy. Sure, I'd had my hand shaken and my back patted, and that had been super gratifying. But this was applause . . . and it was a little bit different.

This, I'd recalled (as Teddy's dad gave him an enthusiastic high five), was what it felt like to be a performer. A star.

My eyes had gone to Sophia, clutching her long-stemmed roses and beaming at her friends, who'd been gathered around her, gazing in awe.

And for a heartbeat, I'd wondered what it might be like to be her.

The feeling had gone as soon as it had come. I had given the stars their chances to *be* stars. Sure, there had been bumps in the road, obstacles and moments of fear and doubt. But we hadn't given up, and we'd made something happen. Something wonderful. Kids who'd never exchanged so much as a hello before joining Random Farms were friends now . . . good friends.

An abandoned barn had been transformed into a beautiful space where people could come to be dazzled and entertained.

I had had an idea, and I'd been lucky enough to find all the right people to make it happen. Austin and Susan, and this amazing and dedicated cast. Everything had come together because of a lot of people's hard work, but I couldn't help feeling a little shiver of joy at knowing that I had been the one who'd had the idea. I wasn't going to let it go to my head though. Because ideas are important, but they're nothing without people to bring them to life.

"Anya?"

I turned to see Susan standing behind me. She was holding a half-eaten pistachio ice cream cone and a slightly melted butterscotch sundae.

"I hope the sundae's for me," I joked.

"Yep." She handed me the bowl of ice cream, a plastic spoon, and a napkin. "Mom wants to know when you're coming home."

"Soon," I said, spooning the cherry off the swirl of whipped cream and into my mouth.

"Okay. I'll tell her." Susan grinned. "But she wants me to remind you not to be too late. Even big-time producer-directors have curfews, ya know."

I would have laughed, but I had a mouthful of butterscotch.

Susan left, and again I was alone in the silence of the empty theater. I decided I would stay long enough to finish my sundae, and then I'd go home. But for just a few more minutes I wanted to be here all by myself, eating ice cream and picturing Elle and Travis and Jane and all the others, dancing and singing and acting their hearts out.

And as I sat there, letting the images and the ice cream fill me, I knew this would be the most delicious butterscotch sundae I'd ever tasted.

☆☆☆☆

"Pass the sunscreen, please."

I kept my eyes closed and reached out my hand for Susan to place the bottle of coconut-scented lotion into it. I squirted out a drop and rubbed it carefully onto my nose.

"Now, pass the chips."

I heard the crinkling of a bag. "Sorry. None left."

I tilted my sunglasses up onto my head and frowned at my sister.

"Don't look at me," she said. "I don't even like sour cream and onion. Look at him!" She pointed.

I turned to the lounge chair next to me, where Austin was crunching guiltily. He smiled. It was the afternoon following our performance and everyone was in a great mood. I'd woken up that morning fearing that it might have all been a dream, but when Dad handed me the morning paper, there was a glowing review of our show.

It was the first day in weeks that I had a totally free day, and I wanted to spend it outdoors. So there we were . . . Susan, Austin, and I with Becky, Mackenzie, Deon, and Mia, all hanging out at the town pool on the most beautiful sunny Sunday I could remember.

"Who wants to go off the diving board?" said Deon.

"Me!" cried Mia.

"Come on," said Susan, sliding off her chair. "I'll show

you my world-famous cannonball."

Austin, Becky, Mackenzie, and I watched as our friends hurried toward the deep end. I was so involved in watching my sister's crazy dive it was a moment before I noticed that three kids—two boys and a girl—had appeared beside my chair.

I recognized two of them from Chappaqua Middle School.

"Hey," said the girl smiling at me. "I'm Julie Roth. We had science together last year, remember?"

"Yes," I said. "You got an A on the mold-growing project, right?"

Julie nodded. "This is Brady Greenberg. He just moved here from Boston. And this is Joey Garcia."

"Hi."

"Hi."

"Hi."

"We saw your show last night," Joey said to me. "It totally rocked."

"Actually," I said, nodding toward Austin, then Mackenzie. "It wasn't my show. It was *our* show. But thanks. I'm glad you liked it."

"We loved it," said Julie. "And we were wondering if you were planning to do another one."

It was at this moment that my cannonball of a sister

returned to her chair, dripping wet. "Of course we're going to do another one," she said, toweling off.

"We're starting our second production a week from tomorrow," I explained. "At the theater. Ten o'clock."

"Great," said Brady. "We'll be there."

"Don't forget ten bucks for dues," said Susan.

Joey offered Austin a fist bump. "Awesome job on the piano, dude. I play drums myself. And I'm taking saxophone lessons in the fall."

"I'm not too bad on the guitar," said Brady, with a shy smile.

"That's great," said Austin. "We can use more musicians."

The moment Joey said *drums*, I was already picturing an orchestra. Percussion, strings, an entire brass section! And how great would they sound with a whole new PA system? After last night's ticket sales, we were well on our way to being able to afford one.

And Julie from science class . . . I suddenly remembered she'd once done an extra credit oral report on the digestive system of the North American bullfrog. The girl had amazing diction. She'd been really animated in her descriptions and had even made a few jokes about the small intestine.

I bet she could act. Maybe she could sing.

There I went, thinking like a producer again.

As I watched our three new theater members head toward the snack bar, Austin asked, "Just out of curiosity, when exactly did you know for sure that we would be doing our second show?"

"Hmmm," I said. "I think it was about ten seconds after I decided we were doing our first show. It was the plan all along." I lifted an eyebrow at him. "You in?"

He pretended to think about it. "Ahh, sure, why not? I mean, I already have the T-shirt, right? And the piano sounds great since we had it tuned."

I laughed and settled back against my towel, letting the warmth of the sun wash over me and wondering if I would ever tell Austin or Susan (or anyone for that matter) how I managed to earn the money to pay that piano bill on time. I could only imagine what they would say if they knew I'd sold my autographed *Wicked* Playbill for two hundred dollars in order to settle up with the Soft Peddlers.

I suppose now that we'd earned all that money in ticket sales, I could approach the buyer and purchase it back. But something told me the buyer in question would either charge me a million bucks or flat out say no. I was pretty sure Sophia Ciancio was the sort who would drive a hard bargain.

But the thing was, as much as I loved that Playbill, I loved my theater more.

ACKNOWLEDGMENTS

I am fortunate to have had the advice and support of many people during the creation of the Stagestruck series. I would like to recognize the following friends and colleagues for their inspiration, guidance, and belief in both me and this project: Pamela Bobowicz, Rob Fermann, Alexis Grausz, Adam Harley, Michael Kauffman, Lisa Pitliuk, and Angela Santomero; Heather Hughes and Barb McNally at Sleeping Bear Press; Marc Tumminelli; and Susan Cohen and Brianne Johnson at Writer's House.

Special thanks to my parents, Jennifer and Stacy, for giving me the unconditional love and encouragement needed to reach for the stars.

—Anya Wallach

What's in store next for Anya and
her friends? Enjoy this teaser from

by LISA FIEDLER AND ANYA WALLACH

The second book in the Stagestruck series!

I was proud of my cast and proud of myself. But a producer's work was never done, which meant it was time to start preparing for our second show. So Austin and I arranged to meet late Monday afternoon at the coffeehouse to plan.

I got there first, toting my laptop. I bought myself lemonade and a swirled-icing cupcake, and picked a table. Three minutes later the bell on the door jangled, and Austin walked in. Thanks to our day at the pool, his nose and cheeks were just a little bit sunburned.

I was surprised at how good Austin looked with that sunny glow. He waved and went to the counter for an iced tea and a giant macadamia-nut cookie. When he was seated, we got right to work.

"First things first," I said. "Finances."

Austin bit into the cookie and nodded. I opened my

laptop and showed him the document my sister had titled "RF Money."

"So, according to Susan, we made a pretty decent profit." I pointed to the number at the bottom of the screen. "Not bad, right? We'll be able to cover our piano-tuning debt and still have plenty left over."

"Excellent," said Austin. "Add that to the next session's dues and the money we should get from the ticket sales for the new show, and we're definitely in good shape."

"Yes, we are," I said. "Moving on . . . membership." I clicked a few times and showed him the two e-mails I'd received that morning. "Unfortunately, Sam isn't going to be able to be in the second show. He's got a lot of baseball stuff going on for the next few weeks."

Austin frowned. "That's kind of a bummer. Sam's a great kid. And good actor."

"I know. I was pretty sad when I got the e-mail. But I understand that baseball means a lot to him too." I indicated the last line of the e-mail, which Austin read aloud.

" 'I'll def be back for the third show,' " Austin read.

This resulted in a shiver of excitement along my spine. "Third show!" I repeated. "Sam's counting on there being a *third* show. That's encouraging."

Austin beamed. "Yeah, it is."

My excitement subsided as I clicked on the second e-mail. "Uh-oh . . . Sam's not the only one who's 'bowing' out. . . . No pun intended."

Austin cracked a smile. "Please say Sophia's decided to opt out."

"We should be so lucky!" I rolled my eyes. "But no, as far as I know, Sophia the Diva will be back for the second show. It's Mia and Eddie who won't be able to do it. Family vacation. They'll be gone for two weeks."

"That's a *serious* bummer," grumbled Austin. "A double whammy! What are we gonna do without Mia's vocal talent and Eddie's comedic timing?"

"We'll just have to work around it," I said with more confidence than I actually felt. "And remember, a lot of our cast has improved a ton since we started."

"That's very true."

"And don't forget the new recruits. Those three kids we met at the pool yesterday, Julie, Brady, and Joey . . . They've got great potential. And Susan's been fielding tweets and texts all morning from kids wanting to sign up."

"So . . . you're saying our cast might actually increase?" Austin looked thoughtful. "That's going to be a huge factor in deciding on the next show. We're going to need something with lots of roles."

It was on the tip of my tongue to ask him if he thought he might be able to finish his big musical, when . . .

I was interrupted by the jangling of the bell on the door. Looking up, I saw Susan come skidding into the coffeehouse, looking frantic.

"Anya! You have to come to the theater. Now!"

"Why? What's wrong?"

"I'm not really sure," she said, her eyes wide and her face pale. "All I know is that Mr. Healy's pickup is parked on the lawn. There are orange cones blocking off half the street, and the whole clubhouse is surrounded by fire trucks and police cruisers!"

Police cruisers? *Fire trucks?*

Heart racing, I looked at Austin. He looked at me.

We both dropped our snacks and sprung up from our chairs.

And we ran!

LISA FIEDLER

Lisa Fiedler is a lifelong fan of musical theater. She saw her first Broadway play at age seven and has been badly belting out show tunes ever since! Her books for children and young adults include the Mouseheart trilogy; *Romeo's Ex: Rosaline's Story*; and *Dating Hamlet: Ophelia's Story*. She and her family divide their time between their home in Connecticut and their cottage on the Rhode Island seashore.

ANYA WALLACH

Anya Wallach is the real-life creator of the Random Farms Kids' Theater, a not-for-profit organization she started in her parents' basement when she was a teenager. Today the Random Farms kids can be regularly seen on Broadway and in film and television. Anya also created the theater's extensive outreach program, with a focus on bullying prevention. In conjunction with Random Farms, Anya has been featured in the *New York Times* and on Fox News and *Teen Kids News*, and was recognized by the *Huffington Post* for her work as a young social entrepreneur. She lives in New York City, where she runs Random Farms full-time. Visit randomfarms.com for more information.